ODD
ROBERT

WILL LOWREY

ODD ROBERT

Editing by Lana Mowdy
Cover by Rebeca Covers
Formatting by The Book Khaleesi

ISBN 978-1-7329399-8-1

Published by Lomack Publishing

www.lomackpublishing.com

First Edition

TABLE OF CONTENTS

"Man beholds the earth, and it is breathing like a great lung; whenever it exhales, delightful life swarms from all its pores and reaches out toward the sun, but when it inhales, a moan of rupture passes through the multitude, and corpses whip the ground like bouts of hail."

~ *The Last Messiah*
Peter Wessel Zapffe

For the billions.

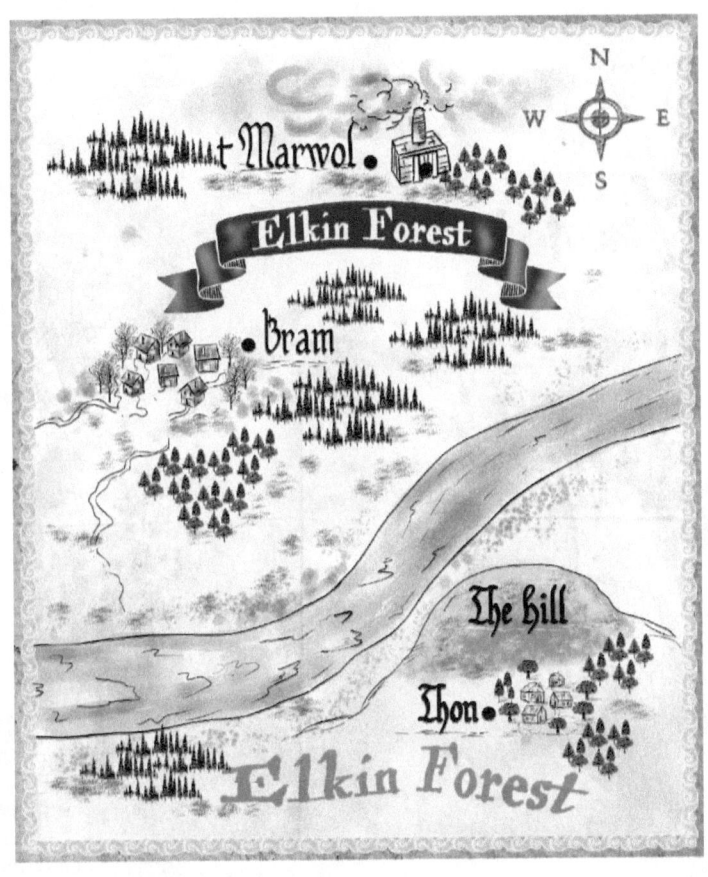

CHAPTER 1

T hey were at home among the trees of the great Elkin Forest. For as long as Cade could remember, they had dashed and darted through the underbrush and hid behind the thick, gnarled bases of the giant farrow trees. These woods and its creatures were their constant companions.

High above them, determined rays of sun trickled through the knotted branches of the emerald canopy, casting a faint, amber glow across the forest floor.

"Come on, Sebastian," he shouted, plunging deeper into the woods. Behind him, the red-haired Sebastian skipped from rock to root, nimble as a skeeve mouse.

Cade veered to his left, twisting his shoulders sideways to pass through the narrow crevice between two of the giant trees and hurried his pace to gain speed before the steep hill ahead. He charged up the hill as high as his momentum would carry him and then dropped to all fours, using his hands like claws to propel himself upward over the dense thicket. Behind, he could hear Sebastian's panting breath bearing down on him just as he reached the top.

At the crest, Cade paused and gazed in the distance as Sebastian scrambled the last few feet and rose to stand proudly beside him. Before them, the forest gave way to a magnificent panorama. The swift waters of a broad river glimmered in shades of turquoise and white as it snaked through the verdant valley. Whitecaps dotted the crystalline waters at numerous places where it crashed against the jagged rocks. Across the river, the view stretched for miles. The top of the endless forest filled Cade's vision as far as his eyes could see. All around him were brilliant hues of greens and sparkling blues. Yet, far in the distance, a single spot drew his eye — a blemish on the natural splendor.

Far away, across the sea of leaves that stretched skyward atop the farrow forest, a faint plume of iron-gray smoke belched brusquely into the cobalt sky. The thick, chalky cloud wafted stubbornly, hanging high above the forest in a dull, unwelcome pillar. Cade frowned at the sight.

The foul, billowing smoke aside, there was little that delighted him more than the spectacular view before him now. Every few days, he and Sebastian would race through the woods only to climb this hill and gaze out in wonder at the magnificent world beyond their tiny village.

"It's a mighty fine view," said Sebastian playfully as he always did atop the hill.

"Aye, it is," replied Cade, a grin spreading beneath hazel eyes.

Suddenly, a startling rustle from deep in the sarberry bushes below interrupted their admiration of the forest. The boys looked downward, their attention caught by the unexpected commotion in the distance. In the thin strip of forest between the river and the base of the hill upon which they stood was a great disturbance. Even from their perch on the towering bluff, they could see the sage-green branches of the sarberry bushes bend and bristle as something moved through them hurriedly, as if an arrow was shot from the river into the dense foliage. Packs of frightened pidgetts startled from the trembling bushes, fluttering their alabaster wings and rising swiftly toward the billowy clouds.

This part of the forest had always been a solitary oasis for the boys. As far as Cade knew, none of the others from the village had ever ventured here. For generations, the elders had warned the clan not to travel near the edge of the river. Few, if any, had ever seen the great billowing smoke that rose in the distance, and certainly no man or boy had set foot on the rocky soil from which the sarberry bushes below them grew. In the village, there was a palpable, unspoken fear of the far side of the river.

"You boys stay away from those waters," roared Hargen, the grizzled old blacksmith and de facto leader of the village, each time they would head off into the woods. Despite his outwardly sour demeanor, Hargen had a soft spot for the village orphans, and the boys respectfully heeded his words — most of the time.

Yet, the unspoken mystery of the far shore drew the boys nearer and nearer. Each trip to the woods brought them closer and closer to the bubbling waters and the whitecaps that crashed on the craggy rocks. In recent weeks, they had come as far as the hill upon which they now stood. The magnificent view of the valley below and the endless forest of farrow trees only stirred their youthful lust to explore the other side. And so, the unexpected and sudden movement in this forbidden place was both startling and intriguing.

For a moment longer, the unseen form barreled through the forest, moving rapidly in a rough, straight line away from the river. Then suddenly, the movement stopped, and the sarberry bushes sprang back to their stoic shapes and fell silent once more.

"Kirill?" asked Sebastian, his voice laced with palpable fright.

Cade said nothing and stood gazing at the forest below him, deep in thought. The name of the great bear rang in his ears, drawing forth tales from the village elders around the fire of the mythical creature said to inhabit these woods. In all their adventures, they had never once seen the bear, and Cade doubted he even existed. *A spook story meant to keep young boys in the village*, he thought to himself.

He turned to his right. "We must see what it is," he said in an excited whisper. Without a response from the stunned Sebastian, Cade darted down the hill toward the river. The narrow, blonde-haired boy moved like a creature born of these woods, his nimble feet deftly picking his way over rocks and branches along the treacherous slope. Sebastian was after him without question. Once more, the two friends ventured into the unknown together, as it seemed they always did.

The boys raced down the hill, grasping at low-hanging branches to slow their descent on the rocky incline until they finally reached the flat bottom of the valley floor with its dense growth of leafy bushes. Here, at the base of the river, the foliage grew thick and lush, the roots of the bushes brimming with life from the waters of the blue river.

Cade led the way, picking a path through the bushes sprawled out under the watchful eyes of a handful of scattered farrow trees. He was sure that no other villager had tread here before. As he pushed forward into the bushes, his slight frame struggled at times against the untouched branches as they seemed to fight against him, seemingly intent to preserve their forest sanctuary.

"Cade, stop!" rasped Sebastian suddenly, his voice peaked with excitement.

The boys stood still. Ahead in the distance, the bushes rustled softly for a moment and then settled once more. A thick silence fell around them, abated only by the distant rushing of the waters behind them. Cade tilted his head and focused. Ahead, he could hear a faint whimpering as if someone lay injured in the bushes.

"You there!" shouted Cade. "Where are you?" he called, his young voice carrying far across the river valley.

At the sound, the whimpering ceased, and there was only silence once more.

"We will help you!" shouted Sebastian, sincerely.

There was no reply.

Cade turned and looked at Sebastian, his expression wordlessly asking whether they should continue. Sebastian nodded, the sweat covered wisps of ginger hair dancing on his forehead as his head shook enthusiastically.

The boys pressed onward in the direction of the sounds. Cade's tattered cotton shirt was soaked with sweat and stained with streaks of bitter sap from the bushes. His knobby arms wore red streaks and scratches from the branches as if he had been flailed in the village square.

Just ahead, he thought he caught a glimpse of something and stood on his tiptoes, peering over the tops of the bushes. He could make out a haphazard path carved through the thicket, marked with broken branches and tousled leaves. On some of the leaves, Cade noticed streaks of dark, rich blood glistening in the rays of sunlight that shone unabated on the valley floor. He turned and looked at Sebastian. His expression took on a sudden graveness at the sight of blood. Sebastian looked ahead toward the faint path in the bushes and glimpsed the red streaks. His eyes grew wide as saucers.

Cade stepped forward cautiously into the path of twisted branches, his breath slowing subconsciously to quiet himself. Sebastian stepped softly beside him then reached down to the forest bed and retrieved a long stick, holding it out before him like a spear. The tip trembled from the quivering of his fragile hands. The boys stepped softly down the path of broken branches, their sandals sticking occasionally to the forest floor from the sap of the broken bushes.

After several paces, Cade paused and held up his hand, signaling for Sebastian to stop. They both listened, straining their ears to hear above the panting from their bony chests. In the near distance, Cade could hear the whimpering again, and he knew they were close. He stepped forward quickly, pushing the dangling branches from the path and picking his way quickly through the dense foliage.

As he passed under the scant canopy of a newborn farrow tree, he drew back the large branches of a sarberry bush and stopped cold in his tracks. His eyes grew wide, and his mouth went agape as his narrow jaw fell nearly to his chest.

Just ten paces before them, something lay stark naked on the broken branches. His mottled, pink skin bore long, bloody gashes along the sides, and his chest heaved with deep, labored breaths.

Cade stepped forward into the small clearing carved by the thing's flight. The stranger looked at him, his eyes like two stones of onyx filled with terror at the approaching boys. *Those eyes*, thought Cade as he approached, still apprehensive but suddenly less fearful. The eyes were deep and thoughtful and shone with an unmistakable intelligence. But above all, they brimmed with an unmistakable aura of suffering, the likes that Cade had never seen before.

The stranger stirred on the bushes as if trying to flee, but his thick legs faltered, and he collapsed in exhaustion as if resigned to his fate at the boy's hands. There he lay defeated, his broken body melding with broken branches, the flight across the river and through the woods having drained every ounce of his energy.

"It's ok, fellow," said Cade as he approached. His voice was soft and soothing. "We're not here to hurt you," he reassured.

Sebastian moved up slowly behind him, his stick still trembling before him. "Can you talk?" he asked the stranger.

The stranger only lay there, naked and unmoving save for the staccato rising and falling of his chest. His battered and bloody form rose and fell with each labored breath. Though his body was broken, his eyes shone with a desire to live as he studied the approaching boys.

"What's your name, friend?" said Cade, now

just feet away.

"I don't think he can talk," whispered Sebastian.

Cade crouched beside the stranger then kneeled on the branches. The dark, reflective eyes only studied the boy helplessly. Then a soft whimper rose from the depths of the naked body — a plea for help.

"You're hurt, friend," said Cade softly, his eyes scanning the bloody wounds that marred the stranger's side like streaks of bloody hail. "And you look scared…like you've been running from something."

"Or someone," offered Sebastian, the words trailing from his mouth. The boys exchanged worried glances.

Cade leaned over the stranger, studying him. As he scanned up and down the naked body before him, his eyes squinted and his face tightened, a puzzled look crossing his face.

"It looks like he's been…beaten," he said to Sebastian, his eyes and mouth twisting into a mask of confusion. "These marks," he observed, tracing the air above the wounds with his thin fingers. "The branches didn't do that."

Sebastian leaned forward hesitantly, still uncertain of the figure before them. "I think you're right," he said after a moment, the last word rising in frightened surprise.

"Go get him some water from the river, Sebastian. Maybe he'd like a drink," suggested Cade abruptly as the thought came to him.

"But...but what will I carry it with?" asked Sebastian, somewhat incredulously.

Cade looked around the forest bed, and his eyes alighted on an old, curved leaf from a young farrow tree. "There," he said, pointing into the thicket.

Sebastian dropped his stick and scuttled across the forest, grabbing the leathery, brown leaf. He studied it for a moment. "This'll do!" he announced innocently then started toward the river.

"Sebastian!" Cade yelled after him after a moment of thought. "Careful by the river!"

Sebastian nodded and darted off through the bushes, consumed by his task.

Cade shifted on his knees and sat next to the stranger, who lay motionless with his back to the boy. From somewhere in the forest atop the hill echoed the sounds of branches cracking and the crumbling of dried leaves. Cade looked up, startled, and scanned the woods. Seeing nothing, he turned his attention back to the figure beside him.

"Where do you come from?" he said, knowing there would be no answer. "And who's been beating you like this?"

Suddenly, the stranger rolled to his left with a short grunt and rested on his stomach, the movement taking great effort. Cade leaned backward, giving space. Then, the stranger braced his legs on the forest floor and attempted to stand, raising his battered body just a few inches from the ground and then collapsing again with an exhausted huff.

"You're not quite ready to stand, are you?" said Cade. He reached over and placed his hand on the crown of the stranger's head, brushing over the thin, coarse white hair that sprouted from its skull. The stranger turned his head now and looked directly at Cade, his long, protruding nose sniffing deeply in the air around him.

Cade met his gaze. Although the stranger was mute, Cade could undoubtedly feel the soul in his deep, rich eyes. Absent his crippled body, he was very much alive and attuned to the world.

Suddenly, the leaves crunched, and Cade spun his head at the sound. From the woods, Sebastian emerged, holding the farrow leaf with both hands as water tipped and spilled over the edges. Sebastian walked quickly toward the stranger and knelt beside him, the twisted branches tearing at the thin fabric of his cotton pants.

"Here you go. Drink some," he said, focused

on not spilling.

The stranger leaned forward and dipped his nose and mouth into the water and began to lap at it feverishly as Sebastian held tightly to the trembling leaf. Water spilled from both sides as the stranger flicked the clear water into his mouth with his tongue, never using his arms. In only seconds, the leaf was empty. The stranger sniffed his long nose at the bottom of the makeshift bowl and raised his head, clearly asking Sebastian for more.

Over the next several hours, the boys tended to their wounded visitor. Sebastian made many more trips to the river until finally the stranger could drink no more, leaving a hint of clear water in the leathery leaf. Sebastian filled the leaf once more, and Cade took it from him, rinsing the blood and dirt from the stranger's long wounds until the scarlet streaks turned pale and pink.

Soon, the sun began to set on the distant horizon just beyond the Elkin Forest, and the translucent sliver of the moon rose slowly in the cloudless sky. Above them, the forest rustled as the night creatures stirred on their branches and in their dens.

"We need to get back to the village," said Sebastian. "Hargen will start looking for us soon."

Cade looked up into the sky, wondering how much light they had left. He worried little about finding his way back through the forest; the boys knew these woods. But this time, they were not alone and would need to take a different route around the steep hill.

"We will take him with us," said Cade, twisting on his knees to face Sebastian. The red-haired boy simply nodded once — he had already known this.

"Come, friend," said Cade. He stood and placed his hands under the stranger's chest, guiding him off the forest bed. Sebastian leaned forward and did the same. Slowly but steadily, the stranger rose to his feet, rejuvenated by the fresh water and long rest in the bushes.

"Will you follow us?" asked Cade, looking back at the stranger. There was no reply. Cade turned and began to walk back down the trail of broken sarberry branches, and Sebastian followed. Neither dared look behind them for several paces, uncertain if the stranger would follow. Then, after several paces, the sound of a third set of feet crunching on the twisted branches filled the river valley. A broad smile crossed Cade's face as he ventured down the path.

As the group began their long trek around the hill and back toward the village of Thon, darkness nestled into the river valley, pressing the last remnants of daylight beyond the far horizon. From somewhere deep in the darkened woods just above the bed of broken sarberry branches, two large, amber eyes looked on silently as the strange procession disappeared into the trees.

CHAPTER 2

C ade peered into the darkness, searching for the familiarity of the trail. His eyes strained into the black night, desperate for a landmark. Sebastian stepped up beside him, scanning into the depths of the forest. Behind them, the stranger shuffled forward, huffing with exhaustion from the long journey.

"He needs a name," said Sebastian, seemingly out of nowhere.

"What?" asked Cade, still peering into the darkened woods.

"Our friend…we need to give him a name," said Sebastian, matter-of-factly.

Cade turned and looked at him slack-jawed. His patience was wearing thin from the long voyage home. "We're lost in the woods, Sebastian. What do you mean, he needs a name?" he said, sounding perturbed.

"Well," said Sebastian, drawing out the word. "If we give him a name, he'll be one of us," he reasoned. "If he doesn't have a name, he's just like one of the forest creatures…"

Cade stared at him blankly, lost at the logic.

"…and Hargen will send him away into the woods," Sebastian finished.

Cade cocked his head for a long moment, processing the words. "Kirill has a name," he said in rebuttal.

"Kirill is only a legend," retorted Sebastian. "Our friend is quite real," he added, looking down at the stranger with a wry smile.

Cade looked at Sebastian for a moment and then shook his head dismissively. "Fine, he needs a name," he said with no energy to argue.

"His name is Robert," said Sebastian without hesitation.

"Robert?" said Cade, incredulous.

"Robert," said Sebastian definitively.

Cade looked puzzled. "Why Robert?"

"Robert is quite normal," Sebastian replied. "Our friend has clearly had anything but a normal life," he continued. "From now on, things will be quite normal for Robert."

Cade stared at him, his eyes squinting in the darkness. He had nothing to say and only shook his head in exasperation. His gaze returned to the woods.

"There!" said Cade. "I see the way," he announced excitedly as he hurried forward into the forest.

Sebastian looked down at the stranger. "Come on, Robert," he said cheerfully, and the two of them moved briskly to catch Cade.

The trio pushed forward through the forest, stepping over the large roots and ducking under the broad, gnarled branches of the farrow trees. After a short distance, they stepped onto a path, the leaves and dirt beaten down from the regular travels of the villagers through the woods.

Cade led the way as usual, walking swiftly toward the village. He had no doubt that Hargen and the others would be upset. Once before, the boys had returned from the woods in the early evening, and the villagers had already gathered to search for them. As the sun set long ago, he suspected they were once again deep into the woods now, worried at what fate may have befallen the wayward pair.

Suddenly, from off to their left, a baleful howl pierced the black night. Cade froze in his tracks, and an icy chill ran up his spine. Next to him, he could hear the chattering of Sebastian's teeth. Beside Sebastian, Robert stood motionless, looking worriedly at the boys for direction.

"A wolf," stammered Sebastian. "He's going to get us," he whimpered.

"Hush, Sebastian," reprimanded Cade, conjuring a false sense of bravery. "He's not going to get us," he said, not entirely convinced at his own words.

Cade crouched down and looked to the bed of the forest. Digging around in the darkness, he retrieved two long, broken branches, handing one to Sebastian.

"If he comes, keep him at bay," he said. "Like a spear, Sebastian," he added, poking his stick forward in demonstration. "We must keep him at a distance."

Sebastian nodded, the whites of his frightened eyes visible in the darkness. Cautiously, Cade continued down the path, his head swiveling from side to side, searching the night for any signs of the wolf.

With slow, agonizing footsteps, the boys and Robert pressed onward through the woods, their ears tuned to the slightest noises. Every creak of a branch or crunch of a leaf frightened them, and they would pause for a moment, ready their sticks, and then continue.

Up ahead, the faint orange glow of torches flickered like fireflies dancing in the distant forest. Cade stepped quickly and then began to run toward the light. Sebastian followed with Robert bringing up the rear, his thick legs thudding on the forest floor.

"Is that you, boys?" came a deep, commanding voice from among the torches.

"It is!" shouted Sebastian gratefully as a spring entered his step, and he hurried through the forest toward the welcoming flames.

Six men clad in rough peasant tunics came toward the boys, each carrying a flaming, knotted branch draped with cloth and twigs. The boys rushed to greet them as Robert slowed to a trot, suddenly hesitant at these strange, new people.

"Where have you been?" bellowed Hargen, his mouth buried somewhere behind a grizzled, gray beard.

Cade and Sebastian said nothing and rushed to the safety of the torches. As the boys approached, the men lowered their weapons, a motley assortment of worn gardening tools and a few chipped and rusted swords.

"Who is that?" demanded Hargen, thrusting his torch into the forest at the figure behind the boys.

In the warm glow of the revealing flames, Robert stood there, alone and shivering. The strange lights and harsh voices frightened him, and he took two steps backward, looking as if he might flee into the woods. In the flickering shadows, the bloody streaks along his sides looked like the jagged stripes of a marsh cat.

Sebastian stepped in front of Hargen, shielding Robert with his body. "This is Robert," he said, somewhat defiantly.

Hargen glared at Robert, his eyes tight and scowling under a pair of bushy eyebrows. Behind him, the other men approached and raised their paltry weapons. Robert shuffled backward and tripped on a branch, falling unceremoniously with a sudden crunch of dry leaves.

Cade rushed toward him and guided him back to his feet. "It's ok, friend," he said, whispering to Robert. The line of men stepped forward, peering suspiciously at the strange creature.

"We found him by the river!" said Sebastian, stretching his arms wide to ward off the approaching men. "He was injured!" he added.

The men continued forward, clutching their weapons aggressively. Cade spun in the leaves and placed his body in front of Robert, protecting the quivering, naked figure from the oncoming mob.

"You went to the river?!" demanded Myrick, the chipped point of his worn, rusted sword angled toward Robert. In the torchlight, Myrick's bald head glimmered like a low-hanging moon.

"We went to the hill!" shouted Sebastian. "We always go to the hill!"

Cade chimed in from behind. "He came from across the river…into the woods below us," he pleaded, desperate to stop the ill-tempered mob from hurting Robert.

The men stopped their approach at Cade's words. Myrick and Hargen exchanged worried looks. Behind them, the rest of the men shuffled uneasily and lowered their weapons, looking back and forth at each other.

"Come now," said Hargen in a sharp whisper, his eyes scanning the forest. "We must get back to the village," he continued. "We will discuss this later," he said, glowering at Cade. Hargen gestured hurriedly for the boys to move past him toward the village.

Sensing Hargen's urgency, Cade and Sebastian started for the village in a run as Robert shuffled quickly behind them. The men closed rank, forming a wall behind the boys. Myrick stayed the furthest back, walking backward and shielding the others as they headed through the forest toward the village.

By the time they reached the forest's edge, the morning sun had started its slow ascent in the east, the sparkling, golden rays illuminating the small village of Thon. Spread out humbly in a field at the base of the giant farrow trees stood a dozen wooden structures spaced evenly, including tiny houses with their thatch roofs and a smattering of blocky, wooden storage buildings. Surrounded by the structures was a large, vast field, its rich, dark soil teeming with crops of all sorts — corn, squash, pumpkins, carrots, lettuce, tomatoes, and all manner of other vegetables. As far as the eye could see, on the fringes of the village, row after row of lush trees blossomed, their branches brimming with brilliant oranges and crisp, red apples.

As the group approached the village, Robert sniffed heartily in the air, his nose twitching at the rich scents of the foreign harvest. Behind him, Hargen and Myrick exchanged tense glances, wary of the stranger in their midst.

From the bowels of the humble, wooden shacks, women and children spilled forth in rustic smocks and tunics, rushing to meet the gaggle headed in from the woods.

"You boys!" cried an old woman, shambling forward in a tattered rag of a dress. "I thought we had seen the last of you!" she howled, her voice shrill on the early morning air. She rushed forward and threw her arms around the boys, clutching them each to a side.

"Hello, Brunda," said Sebastian with grin. The old woman pressed his face to her cheek and squeezed. Cade squirmed from her grasp with a wry smile and trotted into the village, turning to make sure Robert was following.

"Who in the world is that?" cried Brunda, staring bewildered at Robert.

"He's a friend. His name is Robert," said Sebastian, not missing a beat.

The boys and Robert continued into the village as Brunda stood and stared after them and then slowly turned and looked toward the men. Creases of worry lined Hargen's face, and Myrick shook his head in disapproval.

"From the river," said Myrick; his auburn eyes seemed to grow darker with his grave tone. "He comes from across the river," he said again and shook his head grimly.

Brunda looked startled. Her eyes grew wide, and her skin seemed to turn a dull pallor. She looked at Hargen, who only nodded solemnly. "We need to get him inside," he said to her in a whisper.

After a short distance, the boys and Robert were in the center of the village. The pungent aromas of the vast gardens filled their noses as villagers stepped out into the trodden path from all all sides to observe the strange parade.

"Hello, boys," said old Sendus cheerfully, rocking in his creaking chair outside the door to his decrepit shack. In his younger years, Sendus had been wild and free, and Cade could sense that the now-feeble, old man admired their adventure. Then, Sendus looked up and saw Robert trotting behind the boys. His eyes grew large and wide. The creaking of his chair stopped, and his face appeared stricken with fear, the cheerfulness dissipating quickly behind his wiry, white beard.

"What's wrong with him?" whispered Sebastian to Cade. Cade only shrugged and continued on through the village.

"To the storage barn, boys!" bellowed Myrick from behind. Cade turned and looked at the group of adults behind them. Myrick was gesturing firmly with his sword toward the large wooden barn at the southern edge of the village. The boys headed toward the structure with Robert following close behind them.

Two of the other adults hustled ahead of the boys, their sandals kicking up dust as they ran. Each took one of the big barn doors and pulled them open, revealing a gaping black chasm within. The boys looked at the men, perplexed. The men said nothing in return, only nodding with their heads for the boys to enter.

Behind them, Hargen and Myrick followed, and the two other men shut the doors from the outside. Myrick stepped toward the central wooden pillar of the barn and struck a flint, lighting a torch encased in a dented, iron lantern. The luminous, orange glow spread around the barn, lighting up countless crates and boxes brimming with fruits and vegetables of all sorts.

Hargen stepped forward and faced the boys and Robert. His face looked grave and afflicted, the lantern glow illuminating the harsh crease of his frown.

"You shouldn't have brought him here," he admonished, his tone dark and earnest. "You don't know what you have done," he said, staring coldly at the boys.

Cade and Sebastian stood there in the dimly lit barn looking puzzled and afraid. Behind them, Robert sniffed at the air, his nose twitching obliviously at the mingling of dozens of strange new scents.

Myrick spoke from the shadows behind Hargen, the torchlight outlining his chiseled face and rough, bald head. "You were not to have traveled to the river. You knew that the river was forbidden," he seethed.

"But, but…" sputtered Sebastian, unable to find the words.

"We were on the hilltop, Myrick," said Cade resolutely. He stared at the rough man defiantly. "We always go to the hilltop," he said.

Myrick retorted, "This *thing*…" he said, the word carrying an ugly tone, "…it did not climb the hilltop." He pointed at Robert, who cowered, seeming to sense the unpleasant attention.

"His name is Robert!" shouted Sebastian, incensed at Myrick's words.

Cade glanced at the other boy, surprised at his sudden passion. "He was scared and injured. We were not going to leave him," retorted Cade. His voice was calm but firm. "We were once injured and scared," he said, gesturing between himself and Sebastian. "And *you* did not leave us," he reminded the two men before him.

Cade's mind was still young and remembered very little of his days before Thon, but there were some memories that would never leave him. He recalled his early childhood in the tiny village of Bram, many miles to the north, across the river toward the great, billowing smoke. He could remember waking at night to the sounds of angry shouting, the cries of the villagers, and the pungent smell of burning wood. His mother had snatched him from his room and brought him close, cowering in the corner of their wooden shack beneath a threadbare blanket.

He recalled the door bursting open violently, the frail hinges buckling, and the bright light of the village ablaze outside, illuminating the room around him. He remembered the large, rough men clad in their leather cloaks, their faces shrouded with dark hoods, storming into the shack and dragging them out onto the dirt path.

His mind could never erase the look of anguish on his mother's face as the glimmering steel sword rammed through her from behind and the final words that formed on her twisted, dying lips. "Run, sweet boy," she whispered with her last breath, and so he did, squirming free from the men's grasp and darting for the forest as fast as his young legs could carry him. The forest was safety. In the darkness of the trees, he could escape and hide.

Cade remembered returning to the village two days later when the men were long gone and the flaming shacks had burned to smoldering ruins. It was then, on his way from the village back into the forest, that he had found Sebastian, scraped and bruised, hiding in a natural cavern beneath the fallen trunk of a farrow tree. Nearby, a giant Sable Hawk kept vigil on the boy, crying a shrill warning as Cade approached. As the hawk let out its piercing warning, Sebastian huddled further into the dirt beneath the fallen trunk in fear. The hawk took flight suddenly on powerful wings and swooped low at Cade's face, causing him to drop to the ground, barely avoiding its razor talons.

Sebastian lifted his head from the hole and peered out into the forest. His frightened eyes softened as he recognized Cade from the village.

"He is a friend!" cried Sebastian as the hawk circled once more over Cade and then flapped its giant wings, pierced the forest canopy, and disappeared into the blue skies beyond. For three more days, Cade and Sebastian had remained in the forest, surviving on the sap of the sarberry bushes and the roots of the farrow trees, which they chipped with jagged rocks and chewed with their dull teeth. On the third day, a group of men had appeared — a dozen peasants on foot in their filthy tunics, carrying pitchforks, shovels, and a few rusted swords.

At first, the boys hid in the forest as the men searched the burnt husks of the homes for survivors. After some time, the boys grew hungry and cold and stepped desperately from the woods into the clearing toward the men. It was Myrick who had seen them first, his hardened eyes becoming tender at the sight of the bedraggled pair. And so the boys had come to find their home in Thon, the two last survivors of the now-dead village of Bram.

From the look in their eyes, Myrick and Hargen remembered the scene, as well. They stood stoically and studied the defiant little boy pensively. The flicker of the torch divulged a spark of remembrance in their gazes as they looked on him for a long moment.

"Yes," said Myrick, his face softening once more. "Yes," he said thoughtfully.

Hargen stared at Robert, scanning up and down the length of his naked body, studying the brutal scars and wounds on his sides. He gazed dispassionately at him for several long seconds.

"He will go in the cellar for now," he said, his voice still firm, but Cade sensed a hint gentleness creeping in. "We must discuss and decide what to do with your friend."

"Robert," said Sebastian quietly with his head bowed. "His name is Robert."

The men were silent for a moment and then Hargen spoke once more. "He is an odd one to be called Robert," he said in his deep tenor.

From behind Hargen, Myrick looked at Robert, who stood mute in the shadows behind Cade, shifting his weight from foot to foot. "Odd Robert," declared Myrick with a thin, warm smile. "Come with us," he beckoned, turning to walk deeper into the barn.

Sebastian and Cade turned to each other; a conquering grin crossed their faces as they started after Myrick, gesturing and whispering for Robert to follow.

When they reached the back of the barn, Myrick struck another flint, lighting a second lamp. Hargen bent his large frame, grunting at the effort, and pushed aside two large crates to reveal a square, wooden door in the barn floor. He reached into his tunic and withdrew a ring of iron keys, placing one into the large padlock on the door and turning it until the lock opened with a rusted click. Hargen lifted the door to reveal a black pit below.

"We'll have to carry him down the ladder," he said, turning on his knees to look at the boys. Cade and Sebastian simply nodded.

"Go down and strike the torch," commanded Hargen, looking directly at Sebastian. The boy obeyed without hesitation, climbing nimbly down the ladder. In a few moments, an orange glow rose from the black hole, the warm glow flickering above the pale gray of a dirt cellar below.

"Come, Robert," said Cade, turning to his side. "We will make you a proper home for a bit," he said with a trace of a smile.

Myrick and Hargen looked on as Cade guided Robert to the ladder. Sebastian rose on the rungs from the bottom, and the boys guided the strange creature to the edge of the hole into Sebastian's arms.

"Here, let me help...," said Myrick.

"No, we can do this," said Cade stubbornly as

he held on to Robert's arms and began to lower him down the ladder. Sebastian climbed downward, bearing Robert's weight. Robert lay limp, with little choice but to trust the boys. His dark eyes scanned anxiously between Myrick and Hargen as they looked on, seemingly amused at the boys' tenacity.

Suddenly, Robert's arms slipped from Cade, and his weight pressed fully downward. Sebastian lost his footing on the ladder, and Robert tumbled down upon him, sending them both crashing to the hard dirt floor below. Robert expelled a sharp snort-grunt as he crashed to the bottom, his sudden landing cushioned by the small boy beneath him. He rolled and spun to his feet, shaking the dirt from his wiry hair in a great puff. Sebastian choked at the dusty cloud and then leaned up on his elbows and began to laugh heartily. At the sound, Cade's horror-stricken face turned to a smile, and he began to giggle. Hargen peered into the hole and simply shook his head at the folly.

Without a word, Myrick walked to one corner of the barn and retrieved a bale of hay, dragging it to the lip of the trap door.

"Make a soft bed for Odd Robert," he said, taking apparent delight in the newly christened name. He slid the bale of straw through the hole, and it thumped on the dirt floor beside Sebastian and Robert. "Then come out," he said as it landed.

"We will stay the night with Robert," said Cade. Myrick looked at him incredulously.

"There's no need for you to sleep in the cellar," said Hargen. Sebastian peered up from the hole, unable to see Hargen beyond the edges of the opening.

"But we would like to," said Cade. "To make sure that he is alright," he added.

Hargen peered down into the hole at Sebastian. The boy nodded his head in agreement with Cade. Myrick sighed and looked at Hargen, who only shrugged. "Alright, boys — just this one night," he said.

Cade glanced down the hole at Sebastian and grinned. "Thank you," he said to Hargen as he climbed down into the dusty cellar.

When Cade was down, Hargen closed the trap, replaced the lock, and slid the wooden crates back over the square door. He kicked the piles that had risen with the sliding of the crates flat and blew out the lamp then turned to follow Myrick back into the village.

"Goodnight, Odd Robert," he said quietly to himself as he latched the barn doors closed.

CHAPTER 3

O n the third day after Robert arrived in the village, Hargen lifted the hatch and peered down into the shadowy hole. Faint dustings of sunlight crept in through the open barn door and trickled through the small opening, casting a warm glow on the cellar floor. Cade, Sebastian, and Robert rested peacefully on beds of straw. The boys had passed the majority of their time in the cellar over the past three days, only sparingly leaving for the comforts above. Each night, one would keep Robert company while the other tended to their compulsory chores in the village. In the mornings, the boys would bring Robert buckets of fresh, red apples and thick cornstalks, which he ate hungrily and then lapped down with fresh water from a wooden bucket. The dank musk of the cellar receded before the rich, pungent smell of Thon's harvest.

ODD ROBERT

While Robert said nothing during these three days, the boys grew comfortable with the realization that their new friend was mute. Though he uttered no syllables, Robert proved himself more than capable of communicating with a depth of language unhindered by the absence of words. Without speaking, he emanated a profound sentience. When one of the boys would return from the village, his irises seemed to sparkle with an unmistakable sense of affection. Each night the boys rose to blow out the torch for the night, Robert's eyes followed them, lingering for just a moment on their faces in a visage of gratitude. At night, Robert would nuzzle against the boys, the warmth of his body radiating with rich and meaningful life.

To pass the time in the cellar, the boys would wrestle and play with Robert. His size and strength was more than a match for both of them. For hours on end, they would toss and tumble across the cellar floor until Robert would snort and cough great clouds of dust or the boys would wheeze then giggle with exhaustion. When it was time for sleep, the boys would sit with Robert on the beds of straw and recount stories from their adventures in the woods. They wove tales of climbing the branches of the great farrow trees like the bacoons with their gangly arms and dark, striped tails. They regaled Robert with stories of the time they crouched low in their secret cave, shivering and wet as an autumn monsoon pushed through the river valley, gales of wind lashing the mighty farrow branches like twigs. And they told him of the first time they discovered the hill and the moment their eyes first absorbed the full splendor of the Elkin Forest. Through each story, Robert watched them, studying their mouths in the dim light, engrossed in their every word. Robert seemed to live for their companionship.

"Boys," said Hargen from the open hatch, "let's bring Odd Robert out into the village. He could use some sunlight."

Cade and Sebastian looked at each other quizzically. Robert had not left the dingy cellar since they had arrived. This was quite unexpected.

"Robert can come out now?" said Sebastian in genuine surprise.

"Yes, I think it's safe," replied Hargen. Sebastian glanced at Cade, looking pleased at this new development.

With some effort, the boys pushed and strained and managed to get Robert back up the ladder, his thick legs clumsily stepping up each rung. It was clear that Robert had never climbed a ladder or perhaps ever lived in civilization before. When he reached the top, Sebastian clambered up behind him, followed by Cade, who blew out the fading torch in the cellar and climbed the ladder to join them.

Robert shook vigorously from side to side, and a puff of dust rose in the air from his dappled skin. Hargen coughed and hacked as the small cloud of dirt bloomed and rested on his shaggy beard.

"Maybe he needs to go back in the cellar after all," he said dryly, a faint smile barely visible. The boys grinned at each other. Sebastian reached down and patted Robert fondly on his wide back. Robert looked up at him, mouth open in a broad smile.

"We have a place for Odd Robert. I think he will be happy there," said Hargen as he strode toward the open barn door with purpose. "Follow me." Cade and Sebastian followed without question.

Hargen led the way through the barn and out into the brilliant light of day. All around Thon, the villagers toiled away at their work as shafts of golden sunlight bathed the village. In the fields, men and women clad in dull brown and gray smocks tilled and chipped at the gardens, diligently planting crops and digging weeds. In the orchards, small children darted back and forth carrying buckets of apples and oranges to watchful adults nearby.

As the group emerged from the barn and walked through the village, the villagers stopped their chores, rakes and picks frozen on their shoulders, and looked at the odd spectacle. They had never seen someone like Robert. As the strange procession continued down the path, smiles creased the faces of the villagers. Robert seemed to smile back at them, reveling in his warmth of their welcome. He stepped after the boys with a joyous gait in his walk.

"Hello, Odd Robert!" shouted the gaunt, lanky Norville from the porch of his dilapidated shack, waving with a broom in his hand.

At the sight of Robert, the children dropped their buckets and came running from the orchards, circling around him with a happy, nervous chatter. Robert craned his head as he walked, looking at each of them, his mouth wide with an exuberant pant. He picked up his legs higher as the children circled around him and seemed to be trotting through town as if the prize of his own parade. His wise, dark eyes shone with a buoyant jubilance that belied the deep, crusted scars that ran the length of his sides.

"Don't scare him now, children," said Myrick, having approached from behind. His tone was authoritative and serious as always, but the edge was noticeably softer now.

The children reached their small hands over Robert and touched his faint pink skin, enthralled with the strange creature before them. Little boys in tattered knickers and girls in bland, cotton dresses beamed and smiled at the fat, naked figure shambling through their village. One giggling girl leaned over Robert and placed a bright yellow-black sunflower behind his ear. Robert raised his head as she did, his nose sniffing happily at her tiny arm. His eyes were bright and alive at the attention. All around him, the children laughed merrily at the wondrous visitor with the pretty flower behind his ear.

"You're so pretty, Odd Robert," cried the little girl in her lilting voice, admiring the flower, as the others tittered around her. Broad smiles grew on the faces of Cade and Sebastian, basking in the joy Robert had brought to the village.

"Children, run back to your errands now," said Hargen firmly. "We must get Odd Robert settled into his new home." Myrick extended his arms to each side, gently guiding the children away from Robert. The children stopped their march at Myrick's gesture then bade Robert farewell with broad, innocent smiles, skipping happily back to the orchard.

As the procession crossed the center of the village, they approached one of the many non-descript shacks that ringed the communal gardens. On the porch of the weathered shack, in a large, wooden rocking chair, a middle-aged woman sat stoically. Her long, brown hair flowed over a dull gray dress and draped over her meek shoulders. Across the left side of her face, a grisly scar stretched vertically up her cheek and over the empty socket where once an eye had been. Her other eye was a deep, crystal blue, the color of the skies over the Elkin Forest. The woman sat watchfully as the group approached, rocking slowly in her chair with her bony hands folded on her lap. She seemed to be studying them closely.

"Anora," said Myrick, his tone unusually gentle and patient. "This is Odd Robert," he added, waving one hand at the figure beside him.

Anora's lone eye focused intently on Robert as he drew near. Cade thought he noticed an almost imperceptible wince cross her face as Robert approached her stoop. In their time at the village, Cade and Sebastian had interacted very little with Anora. Most days, she sat somberly in her chair, rocking silently and speaking very little to anyone. In fact, Cade could never recall having seen the strange woman ever smile. Though Hargen had spoken very little of her to the boys, it was widely known in the village that she had come here from the North many years before. According to the whispered tales that flowered among the villagers like crops in the garden, a woodcutting party had stumbled across her, wandering through the farrow trees alongside a small pack of sylvan deer, muttering incoherently to herself. The people of Thon had taken her in, as they always did with the misfits and the outcasts from elsewhere. It was the way of Hargen and his people to be welcoming, forgiving, and open to all sorts.

"The bounties of Thon are gifts to all with good hearts," Hargen would say to the boys each time a stranger was welcomed to the village. "If the creatures of these woods trust her, then her heart is good," he had said conclusively when Anora first arrived. The words stuck with Cade, and he knew that same reasoning is what had brought him and Sebastian here.

And so the strange woman was welcomed in Thon. The horrors of her past, obvious from the brutal scar that marked her face, were unknown yet unimportant. After some time in the village, it became apparent that Anora possessed a strange kinship with the woodland creatures. From time to time, the village children would bring her fledgling pidgetts with broken wings from the forest or furry gray khorbits who had lost their grips and fallen from towering trees. She would mend their wings and heal their wounds with a curious salve from the calendula flowers and release them back to the woods, strong and restored, with nary a word.

As the group approached, Cade sensed no apprehension in Robert; he seemed almost at ease around the woman. Without prompting, Robert meandered ahead of the group, waddling toward Anora and nuzzling his nose into the folds of her tattered dress. She reached forward thoughtfully with a slender, bony hand and rested it softly on his back. Her lone eye closed, and she grew still and quiet, no longer rocking in her chair. From a respectful distance, the men and boys watched.

After a moment of stillness, Anora suddenly shuddered; her whole body trembled and quivered. Her single eye opened wide, the bright blue iris consumed by a troubled sea of white. She pulled her hand away from Robert suddenly as if she had touched a scalding kettle. Robert stood before her, scratching his head on the corner of the wooden chair, oblivious.

Cade startled and looked at Anora, who appeared as if she had just seen a phantom. The sun-burned color had drained from her, leaving her face blanched and limp. A bead of moisture formed at the corner of her eye and rolled gently down her cheek. She gasped once and then collected her breath, looking down at Robert. It was if her touch had drawn something deep and painful from within Robert that had struck like lightning to her core.

After a moment, she breathed deeply and composed herself then leaned forward and rested both hands on Robert's sides. She stroked the crusted wounds gently and rested her cheek against Robert's face as if offering him some unseen comfort from deep within her. Then, she looked up at Hargen and simply nodded, as if acknowledging acceptance of the strange creature.

Myrick glanced at Hargen, and the men exchanged an almost imperceptible, puzzled look. The depth of emotions in the greeting had been unexpected, yet it was clear that they had brought Robert to the right home.

All morning, the villagers labored in the gardens under the unrelenting sun. Trusting that Robert was in good hands, Sebastian ran to the orchards to pick fruits with the other children. Meanwhile, Cade followed Hargen to the blacksmith's shack. The old man said he had some shovels to mend and asked the boy to come along.

"Cade," he said as he settled down at the forge on the thick, wooden stool. "What do you see from the hilltop?"

Cade looked at the old man, confused. "What

do you mean, Hargen?" he asked.

The old man stirred the coals with an iron poker. "In the distance…what do you see?"

Cade thought for a moment, and then the answer to Hargen's question dawned on him. "We saw smoke. Rising above the forest," he answered, his response almost a question in itself.

"Yes," said Hargen, drawing out the word.

"What…what is it?" asked Cade, stammering out the question.

Hargen was silent for a moment then spoke. "Marwol," he said grimly.

"What is Marwol?" asked the boy.

Hargen stirred at the coals and said nothing for a long moment. Waves of heat rose to the sky from the forge, twisting and bending the air around them.

"It is quite different than here," he finally replied, cryptically.

Cade stared into the forge as if the answers to his unspoken questions lay within the fire. The old man stirred once more and flickers of red embers rose in the air then fell again amongst the orange coals. The glow of the forge illuminated Hargen's solemn expression.

"No one from this village has been to Marwol…" he said, letting the words hang in the air, "…besides Anora."

Cade said nothing, enraptured. The magnitude of the moment was not lost on him. Since his early days in the village, he had wondered of the world beyond the river.

"We found her wandering in the woods one day," said Hargen, starting again.

"Yes, yes. I know," replied Cade quietly.

"She had fled Marwol when she was old enough to know," continued Hargen.

"*Know* what, Hargen?" asked the boy, a gentle hint of impatience creeping into his tone. Hargen cast a sidelong look at him, and Cade looked down into the dirt, embarrassed.

"There are very dark things in Marwol, boy. It's best that you two never go near that river again," Hargen replied ominously after a pause.

Cade continued to stare into the fire as the words resonated in his ears. He had never heard the name Marwol before this day. Although the elders often spoke of the river and the dangers on the other side, the great secret across the waters had never had a name. Now, with a name, the secret seemed very real and tangible. Cade longed for more.

"What goes on in....?" he started, but the question was suddenly interrupted by the frantic shouts of Sebastian outside the forge.

"Hargen! Hargen!" Sebastian bellowed from

somewhere outside the door. "Someone is coming in a machine!" he cried, rushing into the shack.

Outside, a discordant cacophony of metal gears grinding and the shrill cries of smoke whistling grew louder, drowning out the din of frightened villagers scurrying from the fields.

Hargen leapt from his stool and raced to the door. Cade followed and ducked under his arms, stepping out into the sunlight. To the north, coming down the narrow path through the woods was a most bizarre sight. From the forest's edge, an extraordinary machine rolled menacingly toward the village, its large, wooden wheels carrying two men seated on a platform behind a giant smokestack that bellowed plumes of dull white smoke into the pristine blue sky.

Hargen looked down at Sebastian. "Get to Anora! She and Robert must be hidden!" he blustered. "Immediately!"

Even in the terror of the moment, Cade noticed that Hargen had only called him "Robert." In the face of this freakish contraption rolling toward the village, even Robert was no longer "odd."

Without any questions, Sebastian raced off down the path toward Anora's shack, his small feet pounding the dirt path as he hurried away.

"Get in the shack," huffed Hargen, pushing Cade back through the doorway with his right arm. Once Cade was through the doorway, the old man reached into the shack and grabbed the squared hilt of a long, iron sword and stepped out into the pathway to meet these unwelcome visitors. Cade positioned himself in the corner of the shack so that he could still see the scene outside unfold.

The noise of the great machine grew louder, almost deafening. The blare of the smokestack whistling and the clamor of metal gears shook the blacksmith's shack at its very foundation. Cade worried that the timbers might fall to the ground around him, leaving him buried in a wooden heap. He peered out the open doorway of the shack and saw a great cloud of dust swirling around Hargen, who stood tall in the middle of the path like a defiant sentinel, brandishing his longsword. Next to Hargen was the ever-loyal Myrick, also clutching a short, rusted sword tightly by his side. Behind the two men, a dozen frightened villagers stood on unsteady legs, armed only with rounded shovels and garden tools.

At the sight of the quivering villagers, Cade knew he could not hide from the confrontation. He darted from the shed and took up position behind the men, armed only with the hot iron from Hargen's forge.

The great machine rolled to a halt just feet before Hargen, its wooden wheels grinding plumes of dust in the dirt path. The men coughed and wheezed at the clouds of dirt and foul-smelling smoke from the chimney. When the clouds had settled, Cade peered around the men and gawked at the strange machine in all its glory. The great iron smokestack rose at least fifteen feet off the ground, attached to the bed of a flat, wooden wagon that stood at eye level with Hargen. In the bed of the wagon were four rusted, iron cages, and on the front sat two ill-tempered men on a long wooden bench, one who clutched a large, round wheel.

As the wheels of the machine ground into the dirt, the wagon plumed two more billows of smoke, and then the engine stopped, clunking and sputtering until the cursed noises gave way to a menacing silence. The air grew still, but Cade's ears pounded in his skull from the echoes of the raucous noise. High above the crowd, the wagon's passenger rose from his seat, towering over the villagers as if a priest from a pulpit. In a swiftness belying the lumbering machine upon which he rode, he grasped the edge of the bench and swung his legs over the side, dropping to the ground with a heavy thud.

Cade could feel Hargen and Myrick tensing as the man approached. On the wagon, the driver sat watchfully from his perch, his chiseled, dark features cloaked in a grim countenance behind a pair of thick goggles.

Cade peeked around the villagers and their faltering bravery to get a good look at the other man who now approached on foot. In his scant few years in this world, he had never seen a man so large. He stood nearly a head taller than Hargen, and his broad, barrel chest was covered only by a long, leather apron that hung nearly to his feet, spattered with dark, crimson stains. A coarse, black beard sprouted angrily from his jutting chin, and his mouth looked like a twisted, bitter scar. As he approached, he lifted a thick pair of goggles to his soot-stained forehead, revealing a pair of cold, dead eyes, the color of pine resin. He looked insolently upon the villagers. At his side, a long cleaver glimmered under the forest sun, swinging ominously as he approached.

"Are you the mayor of this village?" he hissed at Hargen, his words sounding ill and foul.

Hargen was unfazed. "We have no mayor," he said firmly.

The man's nostrils flared, and he gnawed his bottom lip for a moment like some hungry animal. "What kind of village has no mayor?" he growled, looming over Hargen with a look of contempt.

Hargen said nothing and stared straight up at

the man, unshaken. From the wagon, the other man shifted in his seat as if preparing to join his companion on the ground.

"If you have some issue with this village, I'm the man to talk to," said Hargen finally. Cade exhaled, unaware he had been holding his breath. The iron poker shivered in his hand.

"Well," said the man with the cleaver with a grim satisfaction, "now we're getting somewhere."

"What do you want?" said Myrick, stepping forward, shoulder to shoulder with Hargen.

The stranger turned and looked at Myrick. His thick, muscular arms tensed and rippled briefly as if he might strike Myrick for the infraction, but then just as quickly, they relaxed.

"My name is Deacon," he said. "I..." he started, scanning the village slowly, the shacks and gardens consumed in his gaze, "...seem to have...lost *something*," he said with a smile, his eyes boring straight into Hargen as he finished.

Hargen returned his gaze stoically, saying nothing.

"A little friend of ours...has gotten loose," said Deacon, looking now at Myrick. "You haven't seen him around these parts, now have you?" he asked, an accusation masked as a question.

Cade shivered and subconsciously took a

small step backward, cowering behind one of the villagers. At the motion, Deacon looked up over Myrick's shoulder. His gaze cut through the crowd and fell upon Cade with a sudden weight.

"The boy," he snarled, staring through the villagers. "Perhaps the boy has seen our friend," he said as a crooked grin crossed his weathered face.

Hargen stepped forward, closing the distance to the man within inches. Myrick followed, and they formed a barrier before Cade, making it clear that they would fight if needed. The other man on the wagon stood and reached for a sleek, curved sword on his side.

"The boy hasn't seen anything," said Hargen, suddenly looking taller and stronger than before. "Your *friend* isn't here," he said, emphasizing the word.

Deacon stared at Cade, his intensity unbroken by Hargen's defiance. Behind him, the other man on the wagon drew the blade from its sheath, the wicked-looking steel reflecting the brilliant sun into the crowd of trembling peasants.

Deacon looked down his nose at Hargen. Their eyes locked, and the two men stared at each other for several long seconds. As the air hung with a palpable tension, the villagers behind Hargen stepped forward hesitantly, readying their arsenal of paltry weapons.

After a moment of silence, Deacon spoke. "If you see our friend....I trust you'll bring him to us," he said with a malevolent smile.

Hargen said nothing in return and only glared back at the man. Before Cade, the villagers tensed, gripping their wooden picks and rakes tightly.

Deacon took a short step backward and looked around the village once more, his eyes narrowing like the slits of a serpent. "It's a nice village you have, friend." He smiled and nodded at Hargen then turned and climbed back on the wagon, his muscular arms pulling him effortlessly high into the wooden seat. He drew his thick goggles down from his forehead as the other man started the clunky engine. Once more, the village filled with the noxious fumes from the chimney and the raucous noises of grinding gears. The driver turned the wagon in a large circle, rolling purposely over a large patch of the garden and churning the soil for a moment with the great wooden wheels. The chimney shrieked twice, and the strange machine rumbled off down the path and disappeared into the woods.

Staring off into the forest after the wagon, Hargen let out a tremendous sigh. His shoulders slumped, and the mustered courage expelled noticeably from his body. The villagers relaxed their tensed arms and began to chatter nervously among themselves.

Hargen turned to Cade and glared at him, fury brewing in his eyes. "You're going to be the end of this village, boy," he said in a huff and stomped off to the blacksmith's shack.

CHAPTER 4

As an unsettling evening fell over the village, Cade and Sebastian huddled in the corner of Anora's shack beside Robert. Anora had placed a thick bed of fresh straw in the corner of the one-room structure, and Robert nestled comfortably beside the boys. It was clear to Cade that Robert had never experienced as much as comfortable bedding or the taste of fresh vegetables in his short, dismal life.

The wounds on Robert's side had begun to heal; the thick brown-red scabs flaked at the edges, giving way to the pale hint of new skin forming around the perimeter. As Cade rested in the straw next to Robert with his head leaning against the thin walls of the wooden shack, he wondered once more where the cruel wounds had come from and who had inflicted them. *What had poor Robert been through that sent him running headlong and terrified through the forest and across the thundering river?*

Cade's mind wandered to the men from earlier in the day. He had never seen their likes before. In fact, aside from faint memories of the men who had pillaged Bram that lingered in his mind only as vague shadows, he had known no other people aside from the villagers around him now. Virtually his entire life consisted of this village and the surrounding woods. He most certainly had never seen someone like Robert. While his adventures in the forest revealed a great many strange and mysterious creatures, none of them looked like Robert with his fair skin that looked much like Cade's own and his deep, reflective eyes that absorbed the world around him. Cade wasn't sure exactly who Robert was or why he had come here, but he felt in his young heart that there was something quite special about this stranger.

"Cade," said Sebastian, leaning against the far wall. "Why do you suppose those men were looking for Robert?" he asked, the unspoken question finally aired.

Cade thought for a minute, his eyes looking upward at the shadows dancing on the ceiling in the flickering candlelight. Truthfully, he had no idea why the men were looking for Robert.

"I don't know, Sebastian," he said honestly. He titled his head and looked at Robert, who lay on his side snoring softly in the welcomed comfort of the straw bed.

Across the room in a dark corner, Cade felt Anora stir in her chair. He looked toward her shadowy form.

"Anora?" asked Cade. He could not see her face in the darkness, but he could sense she was looking back at him. "Do you think Robert is from Marwol?" he asked innocently.

Anora grew still. The blackness seemed to draw around her tightly, shrouding her further from view. She said nothing for a long moment, and Cade regretted the question. Across the room, Sebastian fidgeted and looked uncomfortable.

"Yes," she said finally in barely a whisper. "He most certainly is."

Cade could sense Anora's eyes look toward Robert, and the deep intensity of her gaze permeated the dusky room. He knew without question that both Anora and Robert had seen horrible things in Marwol. It was as if the edges of their souls had been carved and chiseled in the shape of profound sorrow, the place wielding sadness and suffering like a woodworker's blade. Cade shuddered at the thought of it all. The wounds on Robert, the deep, emotional toll on Anora — it frightened him to think about.

"Let him sleep," she said from the dark corner, breaking Cade's thoughts. Anora peered from the darkness, the sliver of her angular face emerging as if from a cocoon of shadow. She looked at the boys and glanced down at Robert, sleeping restfully beside them. "He is at peace here," she said simply.

Cade and Sebastian looked at each other and then toward Robert. The odd visitor appeared comfortable as he lay there sleeping, as if the absorbing slumber had erased all his worries for the time. The horrors of Marwol, whatever they may be, were far behind him...for now.

Cade stood and brushed the straw from his cotton pants. At the sound, Robert opened one eye and looked up at him. He grunted softly as if to let Cade know that he was there. Cade smiled to himself, a deep pride welling inside that they had decided to go into the sarberry bushes and help Robert. The village would tell this story for generations. And most importantly, Robert was free of Marwol's horrors.

Sebastian stood up beside Cade and glanced down at Robert. "You will take good care of him, Anora?" he asked quietly, already knowing the answer.

Cade reached out and grasped his small

shoulder and turned him toward the door. "She will," he said as he turned and offered a warm smile to Anora. The faintest of smiles crossed her face in return, and the boys departed from the small shack into the village.

In the sky above, the full moon hung high, casting a soft, pale glow across the thatched roofs of the village. Beyond the village, some unseen bird chirped and called in the forest, and the bushes rustled with the occasional footstep of some nocturnal creature prowling among the farrow trees.

Cade was restless now. The day's events had energized him, and sleep was but a distant thought. He turned to Sebastian and whispered, "I want to see Marwol again...from the hill."

Sebastian looked at him in shock. "Cade," he stammered, "you heard what Hargen said."

Cade stared off into the forest, his mind lost in conjurations of Marwol. "Come, Sebastian," he said, starting off down the path toward the nearest trail.

"Cade!" Sebastian called after him in a half-whisper. "We will be sent from the village if they catch us!" It was of no avail. Cade was thirty paces ahead and moving toward the forest. Sebastian huffed to himself and trotted after his stubborn friend.

The two boys plunged into the dark forest, moving down the faint trails that only they and the creatures knew. The woods closed around them, shielding all but the faintest rays of moonlight that illuminated their path. Even in the darkness, they moved swiftly, stepping over branches and picking their way through the undergrowth from memory alone.

After a long while, they reached the base of the hill. Cade turned and looked at Sebastian in the darkness. The other boy was by his side, steadfast, as always. They smiled at each other, proud to have reached the hill once more. Cade started up the hill first, scrambling on all fours, and Sebastian followed dutifully.

At the crest, they stood once more, looking out over the faint shapes of sarberry bushes and the thin line of forest that ran along river. Somewhere, shaded in the black night, was the place they had found Robert several days before. Below them, the river roared and crashed into unseen rocks, filling the valley with the innate harmony of nature. The moon's silver rays glinted off the top of the forest canopy as far as the eye could see. All above, a million distant stars twinkled at the boys. The Elkin Forest looked simply wondrous against the dark sky. Never before had the boys been on the hilltop in the night. The world look different now as if the whole land lay sleeping before them, save the hidden creatures who scavenged unseen in the night.

"It's quite lovely," said Sebastian, enamored at the scene before them.

Cade only nodded. His eyes were focused beyond the river, across the great forest. He strained to look for the wisps of smoke that signaled Marwol. But in the darkness, he could see nothing. He wondered what lay beyond the river. *What had Robert seen in Marwol?*

Behind the boys, the forest stirred suddenly, and something moved at the base of the hill. Both boys turned swiftly at the sound, their hearts pounding in their chests. Cade's eyes narrowed to slits, and he stared hard into the darkness for any signs of movement.

Beside him, Sebastian began to tremble. There was a great crunching of leaves and the sounds of thick branches cracking under the feet of something...or someone. By the sound, Cade knew it was something large, not one of the small creatures they so often heard on their adventures.

"There!" he whispered excitedly to Sebastian, pointing deep into the woods beyond the hill. Against the backdrop of darkness, a pair of amber eyes, the color of the coals from Hargen's forge, looked upon them, unblinking.

"Kirill???" asked Sebastian in a gasp. Cade

said nothing, edging slowly backward down the hill toward the river. Sebastian sensed his movement and began to follow, the two boys inching quietly away from the watchful eyes.

After a few paces, Cade took Sebastian's arm and led him down the hill. As they passed below the crest, the amber eyes faded out of sight beyond the hilltop, and the two boys turned and walked quickly toward the path around the hill, the same path they had used to bring Robert to Thon. For a long while, they walked without speaking, only glancing occasionally over their shoulders into the woods. Their bodies were tense, and their frightened breaths hung heavy in the night air. Eventually, the glowing eyes were far in the distance, and the darkness fell still and silent. The way around the hill was the long way home, yet better to travel far than face the wrath of Kirill in the black of night.

For a long while, they marched through the forest, their pace slower along the somewhat unfamiliar path. As if the utterance of his name would somehow draw him near, neither boy spoke of Kirill on the way home. As morning gave the first hint of an appearance just below the horizon, the moon drew low and the woods seemed to darken around the boys. Suddenly, Cade stopped in the path.

"What is it?" asked Sebastian with a hint of panic.

"Shhhhhh!" said Cade.

The boys stood in silence and listened. In the far distance, the din of faint, unnatural noises rose from the forest. Cade turned his head and focused on the sounds. He could just hear something far off in the direction of the village. He squinted his eyes and focused on the sounds, trying desperately to discern the noises. Then, he heard it — the sounds of men yelling and metal clanging violently.

Without a word, he turned and sprinted toward Thon. Sebastian followed close behind. For a great distance, the boys ran through the woods, their hearts pounding with adrenaline. The sounds were still faint, but they grew louder with each footstep. Cade could hear men yelling now — angry, ferocious shouts. His heart skipped as they drew closer, and he could discern the blood-curdling sounds of men and women in agony. Through the cries and shouts, there was another, unmistakable noise that began to drown out the others — the sound of great gears turning and the whining of a steam chimney. Cade sprinted harder toward the village, his little legs pounding along the forest as fast as they could carry him. As the boys got closer, the scent of burning wood filled their nostrils, and the horrible ruckus of noises grew to an almost deafening crescendo.

Finally, they stumbled to a stop at the edge of the forest and looked in horror at the scene before them. Angry orange flames licked high into the iron-gray sky from the burning shacks, their thatch roofs crackling and snapping into burning embers. In the center of town, the great gardens belched clouds of black smoke and fire. Acres of crops and vegetables burned together, their scents mingling into an unrecognizable concoction.

Dark silhouettes ran all about the village, their frantic forms backlit by the terrible flames. At the edge of town, the great steam wagon loomed menacingly, white clouds of smoke pumped from its chimney and mingled with the black plumes from the burning village.

Cade and Sebastian stood at the edge of the forest slack-jawed and horrified. The distant flames illuminated their terrified faces in portraits of ghastly fright. They looked on as villagers fled their burning homes toward the center of town. In the maelstrom, silhouettes darted between burning houses, dragging children from their homes. Women screamed and fell to their knees on porches, retching from the toxic smoke.

Cade watched aghast as a dozen large men, their heads cloaked in black hoods, their bodies covered in thick, leather tunics, circled around the scattering villagers. He gaped in horror as the glimmering steel of their long, sharp blades flashed and danced against the backdrop of Thon ablaze, striking the villagers down, one by one. As the wicked blades rose and fell again and again, the deathly screams of the villagers pierced the night, rising high above the din of the idling steam wagon. Cade's young ears echoed with the ungodly, dying shrieks of men and women impaled brutally at the end of sharpened blades.

"With me!" shouted a familiar voice in the distance.

Cade strained his eyes into the shadows. From behind the barn, a sturdy, bald-headed figure emerged, brandishing a short sword in his right hand and gesturing emphatically with his left. He stepped forward from the shadows of the barn into the open pathway by the great steam wagon. The flames rose dramatically around him as if the fiery curtains of a play yet to unfold.

"Myrick," said Sebastian, his voice quivering, yet finding some solace in the sight of the brave man.

Behind Myrick, four villagers formed a skirmish line, armed with a motley assortment of gardening tools. The cloaked men saw the villagers approaching and turned to face them. From a distance, Cade saw one of the men reach up and pull back his hood, revealing his jet black beard and goggled face. In his right hand, a giant cleaver gleamed against the flickering flames, shining like a diamond against the grim night — Deacon.

With his other hand, Deacon gestured, commanding a small group to continue ransacking the village while the other men gathered on either side of him. They stepped forward, weapons drawn, to face Myrick and the bedraggled villagers.

Even from this distance, Cade could see the expression on Myrick's face. His jaw was set firm, and his chiseled face bore no signs of fear. Behind him, the villagers looked less certain. They quivered visibly, their shabby wooden picks and shovels jittering in unsteady hands.

The cloaked men circled around the villagers, their shiny blades dancing nimbly at their sides as if eager to strike. All around them, the screams and wails of Thon dying shattered the night as the other men continued their slaughter.

The sounds of death stirred Myrick to action. At once, he raised his rusted blade with both hands and charged at Deacon, who strode eagerly to meet him. Myrick's sword clashed with the great cleaver, sending sparks into the black night. The other cloaked men stepped forward and fell upon on the frightened villagers whose paltry tools splintered and broke as the steel swords crashed into them. Two villagers fell in the first on-slaught, gutted and lifeless at the end of the steel swords before the shards of their shattered garden tools even hit the ground.

Again and again, Myrick and Deacon clashed weapons, the two engaged in a deadly dance as the villagers fell mortally wounded all around them. Deacon was a full head taller than Myrick, but the peasant leader fought bravely, parrying and thrusting with skill that amazed Cade. For a moment, Myrick drove Deacon backward toward the flames of a burning shack. Then, his sword caught in the crook of the cleaver, and Deacon thrust his arms upward violently. Myrick lost his grip on the sword, and it launched from his hands into the air and landed on its hilt with a thud several feet away. A cruel sneer creased Deacon's face as he raised the cleaver high above his head with both hands. Myrick dove to the dirt and rolled, reaching out desperately for the fallen sword.

The cleaver made a sickening thud as it drove into Myrick's outstretched arm, cutting straight through the bone and severing the limb entirely. Myrick screamed an inhuman scream, his arm torn asunder. He rolled onto his back in the dirt, clutching the bloody stump. Deacon stepped to-ward him slowly, looming above like a great shadow.

Even from the edge of the forest, Cade could see the sickness in his eyes as he looked upon Myrick writhing before him. Cade's breath caught in his chest. Raising the cleaver high above his head with both hands, Deacon took one powerful step forward and brought the silver blade crashing into Myrick's skull, the sound like a hatchet splitting a rain-soaked log. Myrick's head slumped grotesquely back to the dirt, and his body fell still as blood spilled into the soft, garden soil.

Sebastian gasped and ducked his head. Cade looked on in frozen terror, unable to move and barely able to process the deathly scene before him.

"We have him!" came a harsh shout from one of the cloaked men in the distance. The sound stirred Cade's attention, and his eyes scanned toward the source, passing over the mangled bodies of the fallen villagers who had once stood with Myrick.

From the darkness, Cade could see two men dragging a figure toward Deacon. As they stepped from the shadows, Cade could see that it was Hargen. His face was bloody and battered, his gray-white beard stained bright red, and his eyes glazed and unfocused. The cloaked men dragged him forward and threw him unceremoniously on the ground before Deacon. Hargen fell on all fours, wobbled unsteadily, and then collapsed face-first into the dirt.

Deacon stepped forward, his tall, black leather boots striding methodically toward the fallen man. He hung the giant cleaver to his side and reached down with a gloved hand, grabbing Hargen by the back of his matted hair and lifting his face from the dirt.

"Sit up, old man," he hissed.

Two of the cloaked men came behind Hargen, grabbing his shoulders and yanking him to his knees. Hargen wobbled, barely alive from some unseen beating. His eyes rolled up in his head and then back again and strained to focus on the bearded man before him.

"I want you to look at me when I kill you," snarled Deacon.

Cade jumped to his feet instinctively and stepped toward the clearing. Sebastian flailed and just barely reached the back of Cade's shirt, dragging him down into the bushes.

"No, Cade!" said the red-haired boy. "There is nothing we can do!" he shouted at his friend, his own eyes welling with tears. For once, Cade knew Sebastian was right. He stared at him for a long moment and then breathed heavily, expelling his frustration into the early morning sky.

"We only wanted what was ours," said Deacon, hovering menacingly over Hargen. "It never had to come to this."

Hargen seemed to gain his balance, and his eyes began to clear. He stared at Deacon with a grave determination. *The bounties of Thon are gifts to all with good hearts*, thought Cade, as tears welled in his eyes.

From Anora's smoldering shack, a ghastly screeching noise bellowed forth as four cloaked men burst through the door, each of them clutching one of Robert's thick, squirming legs. Robert twisted and thrashed, wailing in a terrible, high-pitched squeal as they wrenched him from the shack into burning night.

Cade stirred again toward the village. Sebastian once again grasped his shoulder and held him back. "No," he said through tears.

Robert fought and spun in the men's grasp. He reared his head and bucked, attempting to break free, but the large men clung tightly to his flailing legs, carrying him away down the path toward the steam wagon.

The flames lapped high into the night sky. Before Cade's eyes, the once-peaceful village had been transformed into an apocalyptic nightmare. Only a few structures remained intact, the rest consumed in pyres that lit the black night.

Hargen looked on helplessly as the men wrestled Robert into a rusted cage on the back of the steam wagon. In vain, Robert fought the men, kicking and spinning as they angled him through the iron door and slammed it hard.

Deacon looked down at Hargen, tottering on his knees before him. "You gave your village..." he said, gesturing toward Robert, caged on the steam wagon, "...for a swine." His lips curled in disgust at the words, and his face bore a mask of utter contempt.

Hargen lifted his head defiantly. His eyes seemed to focus, and his chin jutted forward as he met Deacon's gaze. "And you've sold your soul for a pound of flesh," he said through bloody spittle, the words laced with the conviction of a man who had made peace with death.

Deacon snarled and reached to his side. With one fluid motion, he unfastened the great cleaver and swung it sideways in a tremendous arc, driving it deep into Hargen's neck. The old man's head wobbled and then fell with a sickly thud, rolling once in the dirt and then settling, his face etched in death with an unmistakable look of defiance.

Cade swayed forward on his knees and fell into the bushes, burying his head in his hands. Behind him, he could hear Sebastian's muffled sobs. The world they knew was no more.

In the distance, Deacon's voice stirred Cade to attention once more. "Ahhhh, Anora," he said with sick satisfaction. Cade lifted his head and peered through the bushes. Tears ran unabated down his soft cheeks and spilled into the soil.

Before him, two cloaked men pushed Anora forward toward Deacon. Her face bore a look of terror as if confronted with a ghost she had never expected to see again.

"I should have expected we would find you here...with the gardeners," said Deacon, his eyes scanning the decimation.

Anora trembled before him. From behind, one of the cloaked men placed his hand on her shoulder and drove her hard into the ground. She crumbled and fell to her knees, quivering in terror. Deacon approached her, his hand brushing against the cleaver at his side.

"You're much too pretty to stain with your own blood," he said as he reached down with his gloved hand and clenched her throat, his long fingers nearly wrapping around her spindly neck. The air sputtered from Anora as she gasped and wheezed. His hand clenched tighter, and he leaned down toward her until their faces were even.

"It's a pity you don't approve of our ways, Anora," he said grimly. She clutched his hand with her arms, her bony fingers vainly attempting to pry off his grip. He squeezed tighter. "You'll die here with the rest," he said, his free hand making a sweeping gesture over the corpses around him.

The muscles in his forearm rippled and bulged as he clenched his hand together, Anora's frail neck caught in the vice-like grasp. Anora wheezed and pressed her toes into the dirt, rising on her knees in a desperate attempt to find air. Her one eye bulged from its socket, and her mouth gaped open. Deacon cocked his head and stared at her, admiring the woman's fight. He clenched tighter, and finally, Anora grew still and her body fell limp. Deacon released his grasp, and she dropped to the dirt — her frail body buckling upon itself like some lifeless marionette.

Deacon looked at her contorted body dispassionately for a moment and then lifted his gaze toward the cloaked men who gathered around him. "To Marwol," he said simply — the deed here was done.

The great steam wagon churned its gears, and a puff of smoke rose from the chimney into the last vestiges of night. Deacon cast a final gaze around the village, taking in the panorama of destruction. Then he reached high up on the wagon and hoisted himself up onto the wooden bench beside the driver. The cloaked men lifted themselves into the rear around Robert's cage and clung to the sides of the steam wagon. With a billow of smoke and a shrill cry, the steam wagon turned a large circle over the smoldering garden and headed north toward the forest.

Cade gazed in shock at the backs of the men and the wagon as it pulled away, leaving behind a scene of complete and utter devastation. Through a small gap in the men on the back of the wagon, he could just see the outline of the iron cage. Beyond the rusted iron bars, Robert's faint shape stood motionless, and his frightened black eyes faded into nothingness as the wagon rolled down the path and vanished in the night.

When the sounds of the wagon receded and only the crackling of burning embers filled his ears, Cade lifted himself from the ground on his elbows, braced his feet beneath him, and sprinted into the village. Sebastian jogged behind him. When Cade reached the center of the burning village, he stopped and scanned the carnage. All around him, shacks were burned to their foundations. Great plumes of gray-black smoke wafted from the charred crops straight into the sky, obscuring the rising sun.

A movement to Cade's left drew his attention — it was Anora. Her thin hand clawed softly at the dirt. Cade rushed to her side and rolled her on her back. Her face was smeared with soot, and her single eye was flushed and bright red, the capillaries ruptured. She coughed grotesquely, and blood bubbled from her mouth and rolled down the sides of her chin.

"Anora," said Cade, desperately.

"Ro...Robert...." she said faintly, only a whisper. Cade pressed his face to hers, barely able to hear the words.

"Marwol......" she gasped in her last breaths. "There...are.......others."

Cade stared at her lips, reading the words. "What *others*?" he demanded.

Anora wheezed, and her chest gurgled as he held her head in his hands. Her mouth opened to speak, but the words fell silent. Her eyelids closed, and her head rolled back in Cade's grasp. He could feel the last ounces of life drain from her. Cade leaned her body back and rested it softly on the ground, holding her tenderly for a moment as the tears streamed down his cheeks and soaked into her cotton dress.

CHAPTER 5

T he sun peeked over the eastern horizon and began its slow ascent over the Elkin Forest. The golden rods of light pierced the dense forest canopy, illuminating the macabre aftermath of the night before.

Cade stirred in his den, already awake before the edges of the sun crested in the sky. At times in the past, when the skies had opened unexpectedly and the rain poured forth or the boys had simply sought to avoid detection by the villagers, they had sought refuge in this hidden place. The deep roots of a long-toppled farrow tree, ripped from the life-giving soil, had left a sunken indentation in the ground. The boys had dug further with hands and sticks, extending the natural hole into a small cave, concealed under the horizontal trunk of the fallen tree.

In the dim light of the manmade cave, Cade

looked at Sebastian sleeping restfully just a few feet away. The red-haired boy was exhausted from the day before. His mind and body expended by horrors he had witnessed.

Cade sat alone in the darkness, contemplating the remnants of his world. When he first arrived in Thon, his mind was young and could remember little of the world before. Back then, his shallow memories masked the depths of loss when he fled his mother's arms for the forest. Now, the feeling was much different. The bulk of his memories consisted of life in Thon — the vast gardens teeming with crops, the diverse villagers with rich stories and lessons, and the natural splendor of the Elkin Forest. Hargen had taken him in when he had nothing. Through the old man's teachings, he had learned to be respectful, to become part of a community, and to cherish the gifts that abounded around him — the forest, the land, the crops, the creatures of the woods. In a horrific inferno of violence, it was all gone, lost forever at the end of sharp blades wielded by shrouded men who wrought havoc and then vanished into the forest like specters.

And what had become of Robert? The strange creature had arrived in Thon after fleeing through the Elkin Forest in sheer terror. His thick, awkward frame had somehow incredibly swum the treacherous river and plunged headlong into the sarberry bushes, driven only by the primal instinct of survival. Robert had survived, indeed. But now he was gone, and for all Cade knew, he may since have been killed by the men who destroyed Thon and carried him away.

Then, he remembered what Anora had said with her final words. *There are others.*

What had she meant? More creatures like Robert? Were they suffering? Were they being beaten, their sides flayed and scarred like Robert's? What sort of world was Marwol where men with sharpened steel lusted for the blood of other creatures?

This was not the world that Hargen had shown him. As he sat there alone with his thoughts in the forest cave, his spindly body shivered at the visions of Marwol that played through his head. Somewhere, north through the Elkin Forest, lie horrors beyond his wildest imagination.

"Cade," said the voice softly from the dark. His thoughts faded as Sebastian's voice drew him back to the present. He turned his head to the faint outline of the other boy; the whites of his eyes shown in the dim light of the cave.

"We must go to Marwol," said Sebastian resolutely.

Cade said nothing; he simply stared unexpectedly at the gentle boy, the only other survivor of

Bram and now Thon, too.

"For Robert," said Sebastian, his eyes now bright and clear even in the dusky gray of their lair. "For the others."

Cade slowly nodded. A tear filled the corner of his eye and streamed down his soft cheek. "Yes," was all he said, faintly.

As the morning sun drew high in the sky, the boys trekked through the Elkin Forest, picking their way over craggy rocks and the twisted braches of the sarberry bushes. Cade carried Myrick's rusted sword before him, using it to push away the thick foliage. Holding the old, worn sword, he felt a certain power. Myrick stood defiantly in the face of overwhelming odds with this very sword and fought bravely for Thon. He surely knew he would die, yet he fought with an uncommon valor. Cade grasped the sword tightly, his spirit melding with the simple wooden hilt; he would carry the sword proudly, a tribute to Myrick.

Behind him, Sebastian stepped gently on the forest floor, his feet light and nimble. In his left hand, he carried the wooden shaft of a garden spade, broken and splintered from its metal head by the ferocious blow of an unforgiving steel sword. Sebastian had tried to carry Hargen's sword, but it proved too heavy for the slight boy, so he drove the blade deep into the soil before the forge, pried the broken, wooden shaft from the bloody hands of a villager and hurried after Cade.

The boys picked their way through the forest and up the hill. Once again, they stood in the bright sunlight overlooking the great river below, watching the rapids bubble over the jagged rocks. In the far distance, the plumes of smoke from Marwol rose ominously over the emerald forest, marking their destination.

Cade paused on the hilltop and surveyed the scene. He studied the river below and plotted the least hazardous path before them, spotting a stretch of river between two rapids where the blue waters ran calm. He noticed for the first time that the spot was just near the forest where they had first seen Robert's headlong flight into the sarberry bushes. Robert must have forded the river at that exact spot.

Cade turned to Sebastian, who stood next to him as always, and pointed toward the river crossing. Sebastian said nothing and only nodded. The red-haired boy's jaw was set firm, and his blue eyes carried a look of determination. He seemed more resolute than ever this day, his fragile body now instilled with a great sense of purpose.

Cade began to hike down the hill toward the river crossing but then paused and looked behind him into the woods. He could sense that something was near. His eyes scanned the dense, green forest where they had seen the yellowish eyes the night before, but this time, he saw only the thick trunks of the farrow trees set firmly in the rocky soil. Turning back toward the river, he headed down the hill, Sebastian following close behind him.

As they approached, the sounds of the river grew louder than Cade had expected. Stepping out from the forest, the waters roared and crashed on the rocks before them. In his mind, Cade felt suddenly anxious as the realization dawned on him that no one from the village had ever come this far.

When they reached the water's edge, Cade gestured upriver. "This way!" he yelled to Sebastian, straining to be heard over the sounds of the rushing water.

After some distance, the crashing of waves on the rocks faded away, replaced by the steady rushing of water downstream. Cade looked across the crystal blue water to the other side of the forest, some forty paces across. Through the glass-like water, he could see the riverbed coated with smoothed gray-brown rocks of all shapes and sizes. The river here was absent the white-capped rapids, but the waters still rushed treacherously.

He turned and looked at Sebastian, who stood behind him at the forest's edge. His thin, pale face bore a look of great concern.

"We can make it, Sebastian," said Cade, answering the other boy's unspoken question. Sebastian nodded as if forcing himself to believe.

Suddenly, above them came a shrill, screeching noise. Cade lifted his head quickly to the sky and crouched instinctively. The great Sable Hawk soared above them, its broad auburn wings spread wide, floating effortlessly in arcing circles high overhead. The creature circled twice and then angled its wings and swooped directly toward them.

Cade stepped backward quickly toward the safety of the woods, his mind drawing memories of when he had first encountered the creature near Sebastian's bruised and broken body. As he sought shelter in the tree line, Sebastian stepped forward cautiously in greeting. The hawk angled lower, gliding effortlessly above the boys in a purposeful, lazy circle. As it passed overhead, it dipped back toward Sebastian, screeched once more, and began to fly slowly east down the river, its wings pulsing slowly in the sparkling blue sky.

Without pause, Sebastian began to follow the hawk, beckoning the bewildered Cade to join him. The boys hurried their way along the rocky shoreline in pursuit. Occasionally, the hawk would circle backward impatiently, prodding the boys along with a shrill cry overhead. Before long, the sounds of rushing rapids faded in the distance, and the waters grew calm and settled. As the boys stumbled along the rocks, gasping and panting from their chase, the hawk spoke once more in a shrill, primal caw, flapped its powerful wings, and disappeared over the crest of the great forest.

The boys stood at the edge of the calm waters, doubled over, gasping great gulps of air.

"What was that all about?" Cade wheezed. Sebastian rose to full height and placed his hands on his hips, his frail chest rising and falling from the exertion. He glanced at Cade and raised his eyebrows as if not understanding the question.

"The hawk," said Cade, still huffing.

"I don't know," said Sebastian honestly, gazing off above the treetops after the magnificent bird. "I don't know, Cade."

They stood by the side of the river in silence for several more moments until Sebastian stepped in first, the calm waters rising to just below his waist as he stood on the slick rocks. Using the wooden stick to brace himself, he began to trek slowly across the cool water. Cade soon followed, still turning occasionally to look for the hawk, who had long disappeared over the forest.

The two boys forded the gentle waters without incident, scrambling up the rocky slope of the other side and plunging once more into the familiar safety of the forest. The air grew cooler around them, and the soft wind chilled their wet bodies. In the shade of the farrow trees, they wrung water from their cotton pants and shook tiny pebbles from their sandals.

Cade took the lead once more from Sebastian and started off toward the direction of the rising smoke. Though the trees and rocks on this side of the river were foreign, the boys moved through the forest with uncanny skill and dexterity. As the forest grew thick and lush around them, Cade stopped in his tracks.

Ahead, a frighteningly familiar noise echoed through the forest. The thin limbs of saplings quivered at the unnatural vibrations. Cade's heart jumped in his chest as he recognized the sound immediately — the thrumming and grinding of the steam wagon. He crouched low and moved forward cautiously through the thicket with Sebastian following close behind him.

Soon, they could hear the incoherent, excited chatter of men and women. The boys crept silently to the edge of the forest and peered through the dense undergrowth. A sprawling village lay before them. Sturdy, stone houses, their roofs thatched with thick branches, dotted the lush, open meadow. In the distance beyond the houses, a towering church of dull gray limestone loomed over the village like a monolith, a great black bell visible in a tower that seemed to stretch endlessly into the sky. In the village square, the steam wagon idled, billowing clouds of pale smoke high into the air. Dozens of men and women stirred greedily around the rear of the wagon in their brightly colored silks and furs. Nearby, bright-eyed children stared in wonder at the pluming chimney high on the wagon.

Cade carefully pushed aside the branches of the sarberry bush to get a better view of the scene before him. On the rear of the wagon, two sturdy men in leather tunics and black cloaks stood towering over the buzzing villagers. Below them, the villagers huddled together like a single, hungry mass, stretching up toward the men with desperate, pleading hands. Cade's eye filled with a bright sparkle as the radiant sun glimmered sharply off a piece of bright metal in a villager's hand. One of the men on the wagon reached down with his gloved hand and took the metal then turned and passed a small, wooden crate in exchange. As the villager scuttled away, cradling the crate in his arms like some wayward infant with a precious toy, Cade could see what appeared to be slabs of bloodied flesh stacked high in the wooden box.

As quickly as the villager moved from the rear of the wagon, another had taken his place, shoving pieces of metal into the waiting hands of the cloaked man then scurrying away through the crowd with his own crate of bloody flesh. One by one, the villagers handed their strange pieces of metal to the cloaked men until the wagon lay empty and only the children remained, milling about in childish whispers below the puffing chimney.

The two cloaked men swept a few scraps of meat off the bed of the wagon with their black boots, and the children dashed and fought to claim the bloody bits with their small, eager hands. The men returned to the long bench behind the chimney, and the black pipe whistled loudly, pushing a small white cloud upward to meet its brethren in the blue sky above. The metal gears churned and clunked, and the wagon turned a large circle through the village square, moving slowly down the road to the north. The great, wooden wheels turned smoothly in ruts carved into the hard dirt, and the noxious machine grew smaller as it faded into the distance.

Before the wagon vanished into the forest, Cade rose to his feet and took off racing through the trees without a word, running parallel to the road. Sebastian wasn't far behind. The boys sprinted along through the woods, leaping over branches and pushing through prickly bushes that snatched at their wet pants. Cade was desperate to keep pace with the wagon. The boys ran alongside, hidden beyond the tree line, until their chests heaved and their lungs burned.

Eventually, Cade could see the road cresting a small hill and opening into a broad valley. He stopped just before the edge of the tree line, stumbling to a halt and bracing himself with his hands against the knotted bark of a farrow tree. He panted heavily, and his eyes wavered as he struggled against exhaustion to regain focus. Behind him, he could hear Sebastian closing the distance, and soon, he could feel the other boy's short quick breaths tousling the soft hair on the back of his head.

Before them, the forest ended abruptly and gave way to an unnatural, open meadow. The stumps of trees, sheared flat and dull, dotted the landscape like scarred remnants of some lost battle against mankind. The meadow bustled with activity; the unexpected suddenness of it all startled Cade, and his brain struggled to make sense of the scene before him.

Atop the gently sloping hill that rose from the manmade meadow, a broad, stone building loomed grotesquely, its black-gray granite cast a dreary pall over the surrounding forest. At the base of the blocky building, a wide tunnel opened inwards like the maw of some hungry beast. Atop the building, an enormous chimney, fashioned unceremoniously from sheets of dull, gray metal, jutted indignantly into the sapphire sky. Thick clouds of black smoke billowed upward and hung stagnantly in the air, curdling in ugly lumps over the meadow. The wide tunnel belched with the sounds of grinding gears and the howls of unfathomable agony within. Cade shuddered, and his slight body shivered against the cold of his heavy, wet clothes.

His eyes scanned the meadow below the baleful building. Just a stone's throw ahead, over a hundred small iron cages were stacked in a dozen rows, each crammed unmercifully full of strange, white birds; their bent feathers and scaly, yellow legs poked through the wires haphazardly. The disheveled birds squawked and cried in apparent distress, quite miserable in their predicament. Even from the forest's edge, Cade could see their pinkish flesh, visible through their splayed, sparse feathers.

A dour man in a filthy tunic moved methodically around the cages with a perpetual scowl, picking dusty brown eggs from each one and placing them in a woven basket. The cries of the tormented birds rose in a melancholy crescendo as the man took their eggs. The birds would twist and turn vainly to peck at his hand, stymied by the cramped confines of their metal cages.

Cade's eyes scanned north of the metal cages, and his gaze set on another mass of the strange, white birds, not confined to cages but packed densely in a rough corral made of crisscrossing branches. From the distance, the birds looked like a swelling sea of white feathers; there must have been a thousand packed together between the branches. Their raucous noise mingled with the pained squawks of the caged birds nearby, filling the meadow and surrounding woods with a discordant chorus. Many of the birds in the corral stepped awkwardly, moving gingerly on deformed or broken legs. They fought viciously for space in their dense mass, tearing into each other with their beaks and leaving splotches of crimson spattered on the white feathers of the troubled flock.

To the left of the corral, a movement caught Cade's eye. A gaunt looking man in long, leather gloves moved away from the blood-soaked stump of a fallen farrow tree and strode toward the caged birds, who moved away instinctively. They pushed and scratched away from the man, but the denseness of their frightened mass kept the unfortunate ones near. The man reached over the crisscrossed branches and snatched the neck of the nearest bird. Cade's heart pounded as the bird flapped its wings in panic, scattering loose feathers into the sky. As the man stalked back toward the stump, he shook the bird violently by its throat as it flapped and flailed. In a single motion, the man slammed the bird's head to the stump with his left hand and raised his right hand, plunging a cleaver through its neck with a sickening thud. The bird's head tumbled off the base of the stump into a pile of others, their eyes wide and frozen in death. Without emotion, the man threw the headless body of the bird into a large basket, turned and strode back toward the corral as the other birds screeched once more in terror.

Cade rolled from his elbows and lay on his back beneath the tree, reeling in horror from the scene. He stared wide-eyed into the branches fanned out above him, aghast at how his beloved forest could harbor such dreadful secrets. Next to him, Sebastian lay on his chest with his head buried in his arms, unwilling to look.

Beyond the forest's edge, a cacophony of squealing roused the boys' attention back to the meadow. Cade rolled swiftly on his stomach and pulled himself forward on his elbows into the bushes. His eyes followed the sounds to a small plateau high on the slope of the hill just beside the entrance to the stone building. Two men moved beside a wooden chute made of horizontal branches, long black whips in their hands like angry serpents. Between the branches, a frightened herd of dirty, pink creatures moved tentatively.

They looked just like Robert.

The men yelled and whipped at the creatures with their black whips, splitting their soft, pink skin. The creatures stumbled forward in fear, charging blindly toward the tunnel of the stone building, their sides raw and bloody from the brutal lashes. Herded by the men into the consuming darkness, they vanished from sight, their squeals muffled by the stone walls.

Cade's eyes followed the rails of the wooden pen, retracing the path the creatures had followed. At the far end of the pen, his heart sank at the sight of a hundred more of the pink creatures milling shoulder to shoulder in muddy slop. They shuffled and wobbled with great trepidation, awaiting their turn down the chute to the tunnel.

"Robert is out there," said Cade in a whisper. "Somewhere among them," he said, pointing at the great mass of creatures stirring in the mud.

"Where are they taking the others?" asked Sebastian, his voice quivering. "Wh…what's in that building?" he said.

Cade responded without hesitation. "I'm going to find out," he said. Sebastian's eyes opened wide, and his small hand clawed at Cade, grasping his shirt.

"You'll die in there!" he gasped. The boy's bony fingers dug into Cade's arms. Cade took Sebastian's arms and shoved at them angrily.

"When nightfall comes, I am going, Sebastian," he said resolutely. Sebastian saw the determination in his eyes and knew there was no hope of talking him out of it. He released his grip and sat back in defeat.

The silver moon drew slowly over the valley as the boys crouched hidden in the forest. A cool breeze whistled through the trees, ruffling the large, waxy leaves of the farrows. High on the plateau, the pink creatures stirred anxiously in the mud, yet the men had long since disappeared. On the meadow below, the grim chopping of throats had subsided, and the man with the cleaver had vanished into the stone building. The dark night had brought temporary solace to the slaughter on the meadow.

In the murky darkness, Cade could see the glow of flames from somewhere within the tunnel to the building. The once-black doorway danced with the warm hue of torchlight and the flicker of shadows across the stone floor.

But the night was not silent. From deep within the bowels of the stone building, the guttural sounds of gears turning and the squeals of terrified creatures echoed from the tunnel like the harsh words of some bitter mouth. Cade knew now why this place was so far from the sprawling village; the villagers with their fancy clothes and pious church must be sequestered from the realities of these grim deeds.

He cast a sideways glance at Sebastian. "Wait for me here. I promise I will be back," he said.

Cade's eyes scanned the valley and spied only a pair of men, visible by the light of their torches. One stood sentry near the corner of the stone building, and another moved on the plateau near the pen of huddled, pink creatures.

Cade crawled through the bushes and dragged himself quietly into the tall grass of the meadow. The caged white birds stirred, and a number chirped in fear at the unknown shape moving toward them in the night. He rose to a crouch and scampered away from the cages and past the frightened birds packed between the branches.

Like some nocturnal predator, he moved unseen around the edge of the meadow until the corner of the stone building was just fifty paces before him. He crouched low and sat motionless, watching as the sentry began to pace back and forth along the edge of the building near the tunnel. Cade's muscles tensed, and his legs shivered as he waited patiently in the blackness for just the right moment.

Finally, the torch moved away from the tunnel, and Cade wasted no time. He braced his feet beneath him and sprinted for the entrance on his toes, clutching Myrick's sword tightly to his side to silence it. When he reached the tunnel, he ducked inside and pressed his back to the rough, cool stone. As he breathed deeply through his nose, his eyes adjusted to the darkness. He found himself in the beginning of a broad passageway that tunneled deep into the building up a gradual slope. At the far end, Cade could see the bright orange glow of a great many torches beyond the bars of a thick, iron gate. The palpable fear of the frightened pink creatures who had been led up the cobbled slope lingered in the air like a foul stench.

His ears reverberated with the noises emanating from the far end of the tunnel as they bounced across the stone walls and pounded his eardrums. Waves of panicked squealing mingled unnaturally with the steady thrum of grinding gears and the clanking of chains. Under the din of the machines and frightened creatures, Cade could hear the voices of several men. He breathed deeply and his heart raced as he touched the sword at his side with a faltering sense of bravery. Keeping his back to the wall, he crept down the tunnel toward the sounds. His eyes focused on the flickering shadows on the hallway floor, studying the mosaic of flames for any signal that someone approached. As he inched closer, the noises rattled his ears, and the whole building seemed to rumble under the machines. Painstakingly, he crept forward until he was almost at the end of the tunnel.

Pressing himself deeper into the shadows, he twisted his eyes and peered through the iron gate, gasping instinctively at what he saw. Just on the other side of the gate was a small corral made from a latticework of thick, iron bars. A dozen of the frightened, pink creatures stirred in the corral, circling and pacing the edges of the fence as if seeking some escape. One of them seemed to sense Cade and quickly approached the iron gate. The creature's large snout pressed against the vertical bars, and it cocked its head sideways, biting at the metal feverishly with small, flat teeth. Cade pulled back at the creature's sudden approach. It looked up at him, pleading with dark, sentient eyes for some reprieve from this hellish place. Cade's teeth chattered, and his chest began to heave; he was frightened beyond words. The creature gnashed twice more at the gate and then moved away, pacing frantically around the perimeter of the corral.

Composing himself, Cade peered once more through the gate. Beyond the corral was a vast room, bustling with activity — the belly of the stone building. Just ahead, a long metal track lined the ceiling, snaking from the near end of the corral all the way across the long room. Along the track, a series of sharp metal hooks hung at brief intervals.

Cade looked on in horror as a burly man, his round, bare belly glistening with sweat, opened a small gate on the other side of the corral and grabbed one of the pink creatures by the ear. The creature flailed and screamed then flopped on its side and spasmed violently in a futile attempt to escape the grasp. The other creatures moved away in fear, crowding around the iron gate just before Cade. The man cursed at the poor creature and dragged it out of the corral by its ear, slamming the small gate behind him. In a single motion, he spun the creature in a half-circle on the floor, grasped one of its hind legs, and looped a heavy chain around it. He took the other end of the chain, reached up, and attached it to one of the hooks on the metal track.

The pink creature struggled to rise to its feet then stumbled and fell awkwardly on the hard stone as its leg tangled in the heavy chain. The man turned slightly, grabbed the wooden knob of a short lever set on the wall before him, and pushed it forward with a grunt. The sound of gears grinding began to grow in the distance, and a metal axle on the track started to spin, winding the chain around it and hoisting the terrified creature off the ground. Indescribable noises bellowed forth from the creature as it rose from the stone floor by one leg, bucking and thrashing horribly.

When the axle stopped revolving, the man reached down to a wooden table and lifted a long, thin blade. He reached around the creature with his left hand, grabbing its ear to stabilize it, and plunged the long knife deep into its throat. The creature's tortured howl sent shivers down Cade's spine, and he felt suddenly nauseous. At the commotion, the other creatures pressed feverishly against the iron gate, their weight rattling the metal bars until Cade thought it might give way. A thick stream of blood arced from the gaping wound like a crimson fountain and splashed into a wooden barrel below. The creature thrashed once more and then went limp, swinging gently on the heavy chain.

Without hesitation, the man reached out and pulled the lever in the opposite direction. The metal track began to move, pulling the creature deeper into the cavernous building like a snake carrying away its victim. Suddenly, the noise of the gears stopped, and the winding track came to rest in front of the vague outline of a second man several paces from the first. The creature's corpse swung forward and back at the sudden stop. The second man reached out and pulled a lever, and the axle began to spin once more, lowering the chained carcass into a narrow moat of water that bubbled and steamed. The boiling water hissed as it consumed the corpse. After a few seconds, the man thrust the lever in the opposite direction. The axle spun once more and raised the creature from the moat, its body shiny and slick now, as if the tufts of fur and wrinkles had been seared away in the scalding water. Once more, the gears grinded, and the creature snaked deeper into the building along the metal track.

In the far distance, just at the edge of his vision, Cade could see a group of rough-looking men gathered around a large, wooden table. As the carcass drew near on the metal tracks, one of the men reached up and unfastened the chain, and a second man helped swing the creature toward the wooden table. In a moment, the two men set upon the creature with their cleavers, hacking the limbs from the torso and dismembering the creature until it was no longer recognizable as a once-living thing; only chunks of pink, bloodied flesh remained, ready to be packed and traded for shiny bits of metal.

Suddenly, Cade's attention was drawn back to the corral as the nearest man reached in once more and grabbed another squealing creature, hoisting it up on the metal chain. His long knife sank to its hilt in the creature's neck as blood poured forth into the wooden barrel. When his deed was done, the man pulled the lever, and the grisly process began once more as the dead creature snaked forward toward the moat of boiling water.

"Finish these and you're done for the night," said a gruff voice from just to the left, out of Cade's view. The familiarity of the voice sent an icy chill through his body, and tiny bumps formed on his wispy arms. Heavy boots pounded on the stone floor and drew near. Cade inhaled deeply and held his breath, pressing his back hard against the stone wall. Before him, the frightened creatures stirred and paced in circles around the corral, still searching desperately for a way out. Cade shifted his eyes to the left now, not daring to place his face near the gate. Just beyond the coral, he saw the man — Deacon, with his giant, gleaming cleaver dangling at the side below his thick, muscular arms. He stood at the edge of the corral, looking cruelly into the mass of frenzied creatures. Cade froze like a statute and prayed that the shadows cloaked his presence. He dared not breathe.

Deacon looked upon the pitiful creatures, who cowered under his ominous gaze. A thin, wicked smile creased his lips beneath his coarse beard. "Don't be frightened, my little friends," he said with a malignant laugh. "It will all be over soon."

Cade hid motionless in the shadows for a long time, waiting for Deacon to leave. The moment he walked further into the building, Cade peeled himself from the wall and crept back down the hallway, once again studying the shadows for any sign of movement. He paused at the end of the tunnel and peeked around the corner into the dark meadow. In the distance, he could see the two torchlights bobbing up and down in the blackness as the sentries patrolled the grounds. He slipped from the building and sprinted toward the forest's edge, his nimble feet carrying him swiftly away from the savage building. As he drew near, the birds scuttled in their cages but thankfully made no sounds. Cade bounded across the meadow and ducked back into the safety of the forest, creeping along until he could see Sebastian's shape in the darkness.

"Cade?" whispered Sebastian, calling to his friend. Cade approached without a word and crouched in the bushes next to Sebastian, breathing hard. As soon as his body settled into the soft dirt beneath the farrow tree, the emotions consumed him, and he began to cry.

"Cade, what did you see?" pleaded Sebastian desperately, wide-eyed and seemingly shocked that Cade had made it back alive.

Cade said nothing and simply buried his face in his hands and sobbed.

CHAPTER 6

T hroughout the long, moonlit night, the boys trekked through the forest toward Thon in a cold, solemn silence. Cade led the way as usual, picking through the brambles hurriedly as Sebastian strained his small legs to keep up.

They had made their way almost to the river, and Cade had uttered not a single word. The sobs had coursed through his body at the edge of the meadow in Marwol, purging the raw emotions and leaving only the empty husk of a young boy to pick stoically through the forest toward the dead village of Thon.

"Cade!" hissed Sebastian in the darkness, coming to a halt. Cade took three more steps and then stopped, still looking ahead. "Tell me what is happening," implored Sebastian, his tone flush with frustration.

Cade stood there, a shadowy silhouette under the great farrow trees, his thin form lit by the pale luminescence of the shimmering moon hanging watchfully above. He said nothing for a long moment, only bowing his head and staring into the blackness. Sebastian waited patiently behind him, giving his friend time to collect himself.

Finally, Cade spoke. "Sebastian...." he said, the words grave and somber.

There was a long pause as both boys stood alone in the darkness, their skinny chests heaving from their hurried journey back through the forest.

"So much suffering, Sebastian," he said, his voice sounding lost and distant, as if from a thousand miles away. His chest started to rise and fall, and the sobs welled within him once more. "So much, Sebastian." The words choked with tears and stuck in his throat. In the darkness, his small body trembled and shuddered. He raised his hands to his face and pressed away the tears with the heels of his palms. Sebastian stepped toward him and rested his hand gently on his shoulder. At the touch, the tears returned, and Cade wept, open and unabated. Sebastian opened his slender arms and embraced his friend; the timid one had now become the keeper. Cade simply sobbed, and for several long minutes, the boys stood wordless in the darkness until the tears ran dry and only an empty sadness remained once more.

They sat on the floor of the forest, leaning their tired backs against the trunks of the great trees. After a long while, Cade finally told Sebastian what he had seen inside the stone building at Marwol — the iron corral of terrified, pink creatures just like Robert, the metal track that snaked across the ceiling, the blood-curdling howls and squeals that still echoed through his ears as the creatures were hoisted and chained, the blood that spouted from their throats in rich, red torrents, the grim men hacking at their limbs on thick, wooden tables, and the familiar man in the center of it all.

Sebastian sat among the shadows, awestruck and hollow. Neither boy had ever seen or imagined anything of the sort. Hargen and Myrick had warned them to stay away from the river. They long knew that Marwol was a forbidden place but had never imagined anything like the scene that Cade had witnessed. In the somber darkness of the Elkin Forest, their hearts splintered a thousand times for the creatures born to suffer and die in Marwol.

"What has become of Robert?" said Sebastian, voicing the unspoken question that had lingered with him.

Cade stared down at the forest floor. "I don't know," he said softly.

"Did you see him?" asked Sebastian, sounding suddenly frazzled.

"I...I couldn't tell," said Cade, honestly. "There were so many...just like him," he said. "I don't know if he was there."

The boys sat in silence for a long time, both thinking of their friend, Robert. Visions of Robert chained from the metal track, a long knife plunged to the hilt into his throat, haunted them.

Cade broke the quiet. "There were others outside, though," he added with a measure of forced optimism. "In a pen...by the building," he said. "Perhaps Robert is there and alive."

Sebastian chewed on the words, the wheels in his boyish mind grinding with terrible images. "What will we do?" he asked.

Before Cade could answer, the woods crunched in the distance under the sound of heavy paws. The boys startled and jumped. Cade grabbed toward the forest floor, searching in the darkness for a branch, in the panic, forgetting the sword that rested on his hip. His fingers rustled through leaves and grasped an old, rotted piece of wood, and he hoisted it before himself in false bravery. Beside him, he could hear Sebastian's stuttered, puffing breaths as he looked anxiously toward the woods.

"There!" said Cade, pointing deep into the

black forest behind a stand of farrow trees. In the darkness, just visible through a crack in the thick trunks, a large pair of amber eyes glowed at them. Some creature, hidden beyond its bright orbs stood motionless — watching.

Without a word, the boys began to walk backward, feeling their way through the forest gingerly with their feet. They kept focus on the amber eyes with every step, waiting for them to move forward, for the creature to pounce. Cade clutched the stick tightly, his grip causing rotted chunks of bark to fall to the forest floor. With every step, the eyes grew further and further away as the boys descended into the dark forest, slowly backing toward the river.

Cade held his breath subconsciously, his body tense and still as he picked his way carefully through the dense undergrowth. The amber eyes gazed back inquisitively but never blinked or moved, standing motionless among the trees. Soon, the eyes vanished, fading into the black abyss of the forest.

Cade took several more steps backward and then turned to Sebastian, one eye still fixed on the forest where the eyes had been. "Now, we turn and run," he said. And with that, he dropped the stick and turned, sprinting through the forest as fast as his legs would carry him. Sebastian followed, and the two boys darted toward the sounds of the river.

Surprisingly, in their haste, the boys forded the river without issue. Somewhere in his mind, Cade had remembered the spot where the Sable Hawk had led them, and they crossed the gentle river, wading quickly to the other side. As the moon began to dip low in the ashen sky, the two boys followed the path around the hill they had brought Robert and found their way back to the familiar woods around Thon.

At Cade's urging, Sebastian took the lead and led them to the cave, just under the fallen farrow tree. The moon cast its dim, ebbing glow over the forest, and the boys knew that soon, the sun would rise, giving light to an unsettled day. For now, they would sleep.

They crawled into the darkened cave, wet and exhausted but safe in their familiar lair under the forest. In the blackness, their tired bodies slumped against the dirt walls of the cave, and the tense energy drained from them. Without another word, they fell asleep as the moon dipped beyond the western horizon.

Soon, the sharp rays of sunlight pierced through the forest canopy, inching forward into the shadowy lair. As the sun crept higher in the morning sky, Cade stirred and then awoke. For a long minute, he sat there motionless in the cave, his exhausted body struggling to dredge itself from the deep slumber. Next to him, Sebastian breathed in the soft rhythms of tranquil sleep.

Cade wiped his face with both hands as if the gesture would push the cobwebs from his mind. He arched his shoulders and stretched his back, knotted from the rutted wall upon which he had collapsed haphazardly. He leaned forward and pressed his hands on the cool dirt and rose to a crouch quietly, biting his lip to keep quiet and let Sebastian sleep. On all fours, he crawled toward the entrance to the cave. Just above the hole, he could see the magnificent shafts of the farrow trees stretching interminably into the pale blue sky. He grabbed on to the edges of a thick root and began to scale the dirt wall to the forest floor. As he peered out of the hole in the ground, his eyes bulged and he froze, staring slack-jawed into the forest just beyond the fallen tree. His foot slipped on the root and chunks of dirt crumbled, raining down to the ground with a series of small thuds. Below, Sebastian awoke.

Slowly, Cade scaled back down the gnarled roots, his eyes agape in disbelief. He turned back toward the cave. In the dim light of morning, Sebastian could see the whites of Cade's eyes, wide in panic.

"What is it?" said Sebastian, urgently. The sight of Cade's face instantly dissipated the last vestiges of sleep that clung to his weary mind.

Cade said nothing, simply shaking his head slowly from side to side, staring awestruck at Sebastian. He opened his mouth to speak, but the words fell silent.

Frustrated, Sebastian scrambled past him to see for himself, climbing the farrow roots like a forest mandrill. Reaching the top, he too froze in disbelief. Beneath him, Cade gathered himself and began to climb once more. As he reached the top, he poked his eyes above the edge of the jagged dirt, almost cheek to cheek with Sebastian, and stared in bewilderment at the scene before them.

There in the woods, some twenty paces beyond the opening to the cave, sat the great bear, Kirill, staring back at them with deep, amber eyes that twinkled against the scant rays of sunlight that pierced the forest canopy. His girth was beyond any legend Cade had ever heard from the village elders. Kirill rested on his haunches comfortably, his massive front legs, thick as farrow saplings, planted on the ground beneath his enormous, rounded head. His fur was a rich tawny brown, and his nose and chest bore dozens of gruesome, leathery scars that spoke of epic battles from days gone by. As his watchful eyes inspected the boys, Cade struggled to discern his exact expression, yet he sensed the bear meant no harm.

Cade looked just to Kirill's left, and a half-breath clogged his throat in shock. There, lurking several paces back in the forest, stood a pack of four majestic wolves. Their gray-brown fur blended seamlessly into the undergrowth, their camouflage belied only by their piercing, pale yellow eyes. The wolf in front, the biggest one, looked upon Cade, and its gaze seemed to bore right through his skin and touch the primal character of his soul. Behind him, the others watched intently as the boys stood frozen in fear at the top of the hole. Cade couldn't help but sense that these wolves saw the world in a way far more complex than any human ever could.

As Cade digested the surprising assembly outside their lair, the pulsing of wings sounded above him, and cool ripples of air blew through his sandy hair. He looked up toward the treetops and saw a familiar dark shape circling and spiraling downward in gentle arcs on feathery, sable wings.

The Sable Hawk landed just feet from the cave entrance, its large, razor talons touching the ground softly as its broad wings folded tightly to its sides. The hawk tilted its head sharply and studied the boys intensely.

At the edge of their lair, the boys stood shell-shocked, clinging to the farrow roots and the edge of the cave. Stunned, they looked on in utter disbelief at the collection of woodland creatures arrayed before them.

"What…what…are they doing?" Cade sputtered, not taking his eyes off the pack of animals.

Sebastian said nothing for a moment and simply stared at the assortment of creatures, lost in a sea of questions swirling about his mind. There was purpose in their eyes. The Sable Hawk looked at Sebastian knowingly, as if the two had met many times before. Indeed, they had. Beyond him, Kirill rested patiently, the soft grumble of his great breaths the only sound among the gathering. To his left, the wolves began to pace and look restless — as if eager to hunt.

From nowhere, Sebastian spoke as if the answer had come to him suddenly. "They're here to help us." The words flowed smoothly from his tongue, the tone and delivery cloaking the ridiculousness of the statement.

"What?" said Cade in disbelief. "Help us?" he asked. "Help us do what?" he said, flabbergasted.

Sebastian looked again toward the hawk, and something beyond their eyes connected, pure and primordial, a connection forged from the depths of their spirits.

"Free them," he said quietly.

Cade looked at him with a furrowed brown. He opened his mouth to speak but could find no words. Sebastian simply stared ahead at the Sable Hawk, unblinking, resolute in the moment.

"We must return to Marwol," was all he said after several seconds. With the words, he reached beside him purposefully and grasped the jagged, pointed shaft of the broken garden tool that stood vertically, poked into the soft dirt.

And so the strange menagerie pressed through the Elkin Forest toward Marwol. The Sable Hawk led the way in the skies overhead, occasionally circling low to check on the progress of the ground-based animals on twos and fours. Below, Kirill led the boys through the forest, his massive form surprisingly nimble as he stepped over fallen logs and dipped below the low-hanging branches. All around them, the wolves circled, keeping watchful vigil over Cade and Sebastian. Occasionally, Cade would catch eyes with the big wolf, the aura of his spirit palpable through the thickets and bushes.

The Sable Hawk led them to the calm passage in the river, familiar now to the two boys. Kirill splashed ahead into the water. Large ripples formed around his thick legs with every step. The wolves waded silently across, their narrow forms knifing through the clear waters effortless, barely interrupting the current.

On the other side of the river, the boys stopped and shook themselves, wringing the water from their hair and clothes once more. Just ahead by the forest's edge, the animals waited patiently. The Sable Hawk swirled and landed on a branch, waiting for his charges to resume their march. After the boys had dried themselves as best they could, they looked up at the hawk and nodded. The bird lifted on great wings and soared high into the sky, urging the group onward toward Marwol.

As the day passed, the sun crested in the sky above the trees, its warm, golden beams filtering sparsely through the dense forest. The rays of light touched the boys on their cheeks and warmed their wet bodies.

In the early afternoon, as they neared the village, the Sable Hawk circled backward and alighted on the low branch of a solitary tree in a small clearing. The ground creatures moved as one up the small hill and rested below the tree. Kirill ambled a few paces into the forest, his giant nose twitching to consume the scents of humans ahead through the woods. The wolves gathered together and lay in a half circle around the tree, their vigilant eyes still scouting the forest and their sensitive ears perked for the slightest sound of alarm.

Following the others, the boys stepped into the clearing and rested in the lush grass, their bodies weary. Cade rested Myrick's rusted sword on the ground beside him and looked up at the hawk perched high in the tree.

"What are we doing?" he asked Sebastian in a whisper, still perplexed. The big wolf pricked his ears at the noise and gazed into Cade's eyes for a moment then looked away. Cade had been with the pack of animals for an entire day, trudging through the forest side by side, yet the passing glance from the big wolf still left him unsettled.

"We're resting before Marwol..." said Sebastian. "...I suppose," he added, sounding unsure.

A great knot rippled in Cade's stomach, and he began to feel queasy. Only a small forest lay between them and the horrors of Marwol. The images of the pink creatures, strung and flayed with sharp knives in the bowels of the grim stone building, replayed in violent flashes through his head. He thought of the rough men who worked in the meadow with their bloody leather aprons and steel knives. He thought of Deacon with his great cleaver dangling ever-so-ready by his side, and quickly, the images of Hargen being slaughtered in the glow of Thon ablaze flooded his mind and made him shudder.

He could feel the big wolf observing him once

again, and he instinctively cocked his head and returned the stare. His frightened, boyish eyes gazed straight into a pool of pale yellow. The creature's coal-black pupils looked back at him, dispassionate yet unquestionably assured. At that moment, Cade felt his spine straighten, and resolve welled within his tiny chest. The big wolf watched him stoically. Cade knew what must be done was no longer a question but a duty. Reaching into the grass, he lifted Myrick's sword and studied it, envisioning the rusted blade crashing into Deacon's skull.

Above them, the Sable Hawk lifted and circled once in the clearing, letting out a shrill cry. It was time to move. Kirill loped back from the forest and past the boys; his thick fur brushed Cade's bare arm, and the sensation of contact with the great bear invigorated him. He rose from the grass and hooked the sword to his belt then followed the pack deeper into the woods.

As the sun slipped low on the horizon, the group circled the village to the east, avoiding any contact with the humans. At one point, when a small group of woodcutters worked ahead in their distant path, the wolves moved on alone while the rest of the group stayed hidden in the forest. In a moment, the cries of the woodcutters echoed through the forest as they left their tools half-buried in the trunks of the farrow trees and fled for the village at the sight of the wolves. With the obstacle abated, the group carried on toward Marwol.

Far ahead, Cade could see the blocky outline of the stone building start to form beyond the thinning tree line as they approached the meadow. A pit formed in his stomach as the gravity of the moment settled upon him. He glanced to his left at Sebastian. The boy looked pale and uneasy, his tiny fingers clutched hard around the broken, wooden stick.

The group pushed on through the woods and came to rest once more behind the thicket of trees where the boys had first set sights on Marwol. Ahead, they could hear the sound of the white birds squawking and rustling restlessly in their cages. The voices of gruff men mingled with their cries, and in the far distance, the sounds of terrible squeals carried on the air from high on the hill. The wolves perked their ears, and Kirill seemed to grumble uneasily at the disturbance, as if the natural order of the woods had been grievously violated.

"What are we going to do?" asked Sebastian. This entire trip through the woods, Sebastian had been the more confident of the two. Yet, the bleak reality of Marwol before them had made him meek and timid once more. Cade struggled to find his usual confidence in the shadows of the looming stone building.

Before he could answer, the Sable Hawk lifted suddenly from a low branch and knifed high into the sky, cutting between the branches of the trees with an otherworldly deftness. He tilted his wings and sliced through the forest, arcing into the clouds high above the meadow. Cade's eyes strained to follow the dark brown blur, just barely making out the hawk's form in the sky above. The Sable Hawk pounded his broad wings once, then twice, and glided over the men working in the meadow.

Below him, a half-dozen men toiled away at their brutal chores, lopping the heads off the terrified white birds on rough wooden stumps or poking and prodding the squealing pink creatures toward the gaping chasm of the stone building. Near the white birds, one of the men looked up as the hawk soared overhead. He paused, with one hand pinning a writhing white bird to the stump by its neck and the other frozen in the air with a rusted, iron hatchet hovering above the helpless creature.

"Don't even think about taking these birds, you bastard!" he shouted menacingly at the Sable Hawk. At his cry, two other men nearby stopped stuffing the birds in cages and looked skyward.

The hawk circled the meadow, flying from the white birds toward the corral on the plateau and circled low, as if trying to get the attention of the men who whipped at the frightened, pink creatures. The men lowered their whips and turned to look toward the sky, their faces twisted and disgruntled as the hawk continued his threatening aerial dance.

"Light the torches!" shouted one of the men by the squealing creatures. In the distance, Cade could see one of the men hurry to a large, wooden table arrayed with a number of cruel-looking instruments. He saw the flicker of sparks across the table, and then the sudden, orange flash of a torch lit up the early dusk high on the plateau. The man hurried back to the pens, holding the torch high in the sky, thrusting the flames skyward toward the Sable Hawk.

The hawk circled low and then soared high in a great spiral, as if moving away from the flames. He flapped his wings twice and then skirted low over the men near the white birds, who stared at him uneasily, still frozen in their macabre tasks.

"What is he doing?" whispered Cade to Sebastian.

Sebastian answered immediately, somehow knowing the hawk's plan. "He's distracting them...for us," he said.

Cade looked at him, confused. "For us to do what?" he asked, perplexed.

"To get to the building," said Sebastian. Without another word, he rose from a crouch and darted off along the edge of the forest. Cade looked at him in shock, but his body obediently rose and followed.

The two boys skirted the edge of the forest, using the trees to shield them from the men just to their left, who were distracted by the hawk. When they had passed the white birds, they veered from the woods and scrambled on all fours into the tall grass of the meadow, crouching low in the semi-darkness. The noises of men shouting at the Sable Hawk grew louder, filling their ears. Above the grass, Cade saw two more torches lit and gesturing wildly at the skies. Sebastian rose to a crouch and took off across the field, heading toward the corner of the building. Cade followed close behind him. They sprinted hard, their lungs heaving from the hectic dash. Cade clutched at the rusted sword at his side, and Sebastian pumped his arms, holding the broken wooden stick like a baton.

When they reached the corner of the building, Cade leaned against the rough stone wall, pressing his back into the rocks. Beside him, Sebastian shivered and panted in ragged breaths, terrified. The Sable Hawk swooped low ahead of them in the meadow, circling the field and dipping low above the white birds as if threatening to take one. The men scurried about, leaving their posts and chasing the hawk haphazardly. They poked vainly in the air as black plumes twisted in spiral wisps from their torches, and their steel knives clanked at their sides in their desperate pursuit of the hawk.

Suddenly, the Sable Hawk let out a shrill cry unlike any Cade had heard before. The noise pierced deep into Cade's ears. Although unfamiliar, the message was unmistakable — a war cry.

At once, the four wolves leapt from the woods and glided across the meadow with effortless grace. The men's eyes grew wide with terror. Even from the distance in the dark, Cade could sense their dread as the wolves descended upon them. The big wolf led the way, bounding forward as if he were floating on the very air itself. One of the men turned and fled toward the building, dropping his torch and screaming in terror. The big wolf was upon in him in four long strides, leaping on his back and sinking his long, white fangs deep into the man's neck. His blood-curdling screams echoed across the meadow like some grisly gale.

All around him, the other men fled, some stumbling over stumps or cages of the white birds in their panic. The white birds flapped and cawed with the commotion, feathers ruffling and wafting softly in the air. The three other wolves circled a small group of men, who pressed their backs together in a last, desperate defensive formation. The beads of sweat formed on their long, frightened faces as they waved their torches and long knives before them. The wolves hunkered low, their legs tensed and stomachs almost brushing the ground. They skulked about the men in a majestic, choreographed dance. One wolf would press forward, and the men would respond, poking and prodding futilely with their knives. Then another wolf would test the flank, and the men would respond again, their reactions slowing with each feint. The advances continued in seemingly random form, yet the attack was anything but disorganized. The wolves were deadly clever and coordinated.

After a half-dozen advances, the men were frazzled and stumbling on each other's feet. One wolf lunged forward quickly, and the men reacted, but the wolf stopped just short, and at that moment, another wolf on the far side thrust forward, snatching the bare arm of one of the men in its powerful jaws. The man howled in pain as the wolf dragged him down into the tall grass. The other men broke formation and fled toward the woods, their meager defensive formation collapsing in disarray. The remaining wolves pounced on them before they had taken three strides, and now the wolves were astride the fallen men, their gray-brown muzzles soaked red with blood.

From Cade's left, he saw three more men rush out of the building at the sound of the commotion, charging blindly into the fields with swords and spears. They met the remaining survivors and formed a skirmish line, their eyes brimming with unbridled terror at the bloody scene before them. The line of men stepped forward briefly, deciding whether there was anyone left to save and then, realizing the situation was hopeless, retreated in quick backward steps toward the stone building.

Cade looked at Sebastian with a sense of urgency in his eyes. "We must get inside before they go back in!" he gasped. Without waiting for Sebastian, he turned and sprinted along the wall toward the black tunnel.

As the skirmish line of men stepped backward, Cade ran as hard as he could, his arms pumping and his legs striding through the tall grass. If he could just get inside, he could close the iron gate and keep the men out. He sprinted as hard as his legs would carry him, watching from the corner of his eye as the men backpedaled toward the building just twenty paces away. As he reached the entrance, he threw his arm around the corner of the wall and spun himself into the tunnel as the rusted sword snapped loose from his belt and tumbled unnoticed into the meadow. Behind him, he heard Sebastian stumble and fall hard on the ground. Cade poked his head back out of the tunnel entrance to look for his friend.

"A boy!" shouted one of the men from the group, turning at the sound of Sebastian tumbling across the grass. The men pivoted and rushed toward Sebastian. The whole plan was crumbling before Cade's eyes. He fumbled around on the wall and felt the long, iron lever of the gate protruding from the stone. If he closed it now, he could keep the men out, but Sebastian would be left behind. He yanked his hand back from the lever — he would never leave Sebastian. Cade stepped bravely from the tunnel to face the men, reaching to his side for his rusted sword, only to realize in horror that it was gone.

Just as the wave of dread began to settle on him, a blur of brown fur engulfed his field of vision. Kirill charged from the woods toward the small group of men, his powerful legs pumping hard across the tall grass. The whole world seemed to vibrate as the giant bear thundered across the meadow toward the fray. At the last moment, the men saw Kirill coming and turned from Sebastian, raising their spears and swords to meet him. Kirill coiled his muscled legs and, with one powerful thrust of his legs, took to the air, his massive shadow consuming the group of men below him like a looming thundercloud. With nowhere to run, the men raised their weapons as he fell upon them, his claws, the size of daggers, fully extended and his massive jaws thrashing violently at the air. As Kirill fell on the men, their spears and swords sank into the shaggy fur of his underbelly. Cade winced at the sickening sounds as the blades punctured his thick flesh.

The giant bear landed hard on the men, a whirlwind of fury. His razor claws slashed at them like giant harvest blades, nearly decapitating one man and leaving his head tottering on the stump of his neck. As Kirill landed, he rolled and a spear lodged deep in his side bent and broke in the tumble. The great bear rose to all fours, his face a mask of pained rage. The remaining men struggled to get to their feet. Two of them lay grotesquely contorted, their legs broken and twisted like the sarberry branches along the river's edge. Kirill charged at the men who dared stand to face him, and his mighty jaws snatched one of the men by his neck. Tender bones crunched and splintered as Kirill thrashed his head back and forth, the man's body going limp and listless. Kirill tossed the corpse into the meadow like a scarecrow and charged at the others.

Sebastian crawled desperately for the doorway on all fours as the fighting raged beside him. Cade stepped from the tunnel and extended his hand, grabbing Sebastian and pulling him inside the safety of the stone building. Once they had cleared the entrance, Cade yanked on the lever and slammed the iron gate, which clanked hard on the thick stone, separating the boys from the bloody battle outside. He stepped to the gate and looked out at the scene in the meadow.

With their only path of escape sealed, the two remaining men faced off with Kirill. Cade could see the bear's fur matted with dark blood in several places and a great, open wound showed on his left side, the jagged shard of the broken spear dangling precariously from his flesh. Kirill snarled at the two men; the whites of his teeth seemed to fill the morning sky. With swords drawn, the two men approached, seeming to sense that Kirill was gravely injured.

As they drew near, the men separated and moved to either side of the wounded animal. Kirill circled to keep them in his view, but eventually, one man slipped behind. Lunging forward, Kirill swiped his giant paw at the man before him, who nimbly dodged backward at the last moment. Just then, the other man approached from the rear, his sword glimmering in the sun's glow, ready to plunge it into the bear. Kirill spun again just before the man struck and swiped at him, his paw moving in a deadly, sweeping arc. The tip of his enormous claws just glanced the man's leg and sent him stumbling off-balance. The other man seized the distraction and moved forward, raising his sword overhead with both hands. At the last moment, Kirill spun again, baring his teeth in an angry growl and swiping at the man.

"He can't keep this up forever!" cried Sebastian, grabbing at the bars. "He's wounded, Cade!"

Cade stared at the scene, his heart pounding. In the distance, he could see a bustling, colorful mob of men from the village rushing up the road into Marwol, armed with swords and spears. Their angry voices and the clanking of steel weapons carried across the meadow and filled Cade's mind with panic. Ever vigilant, the wolves saw the men coming and moved to face them, skulking low in a slow circle around the mob to keep them from Kirill and the boys. Above the commotion, Cade could see a small, dark fleck against the crystalline blue sky, circling in elegant arcs and occasionally diving aggressively into the crowd each time the men threatened to breach the wolves' defensive circle.

Then, Cade's eyes fell upon the rusted blade of Myrick's sword just feet away beyond the gate. Startled, he reached to his side and patted the place where his sword had been, cursing himself for losing the weapon.

His head was pounding. *What do we do?* He reached his hand toward the lever to pull the gate and retrieve his sword to help Kirill. At that moment, the great bear turned to the boys, the light from his amber eyes now dim, and unleashed a tremendous roar. His matted, bloody fur rippled in waves across his mammoth body as his voice thundered across the meadow and shook the walls of the stone building.

"He wants us to go...to save them," said Sebastian, frightened. "We must go."

Cade couldn't take his eyes off Kirill in the deadly dance, spinning and swiping at the men. He could see the bear growing more and more fatigued with each turn. As Sebastian grabbed his arm and pulled him into the building, he watched in horror as one of the men raised his sword from behind. The bear spun again, but his injuries slowed him, and the man's sword slashed at his flank, cleaving an open wound. Kirill let out an agonized roar, and the pain rattled through Cade's ears then faded as Sebastian pulled him forward down the tunnel into the bowels of the stone building.

As the two boys dashed down the long, stone corridor, they could see ahead through the iron gate that the corral was almost empty. Only a handful of the mottled, pink creatures milled about, desperately sniffing and scratching at the stone floor for means of escape. One of the creatures sensed their presence and moved to the gate, thrusting his long snout through the bars. The distressed sounds of his frightened grunting channeled down the stone tunnel. The boys pressed their backs to the wall, melding into the shadows as they moved cautiously toward the iron gate. When they reached the gate, Sebastian stretched his slight hand forward toward the creature's snout, hoping to calm him and abate the sounds. The creature pressed his cold nose into the palm of Sebastian's hand, and the boy could feel the rough tongue lapping feverishly at his moist skin. Suddenly, the creature snorted loudly in recognition and squealed, thrusting his face into the unforgiving iron bars, attempting vainly to reach Sebastian.

"Robert!" gasped Sebastian.

"It is!" said Cade, in shock.

Robert pressed harder against the gate as if trying to squeeze through. He scraped his hooves across the stone floor, longing desperately to reach the boys. He grunted louder, a rough, chortling sound that came from deep with him and then squealed, his high-pitched whine filling the tunnel. Behind him, the other creatures heard the commotion and ran to the gate, pressing their snouts through the bars toward the boys.

Robert was barely recognizable in the corral. His once pale, pink skin was layered with black mud and grime, like some creature born from the bogs. Down the length of his sides, fresh streaks of blood red betrayed the sooty color, giving grim testament to recent lashes at the end of a cruel whip.

Cade looked beyond the frightened creatures gathered desperately at the gate. His eyes searched the room for any sign of more men. At the far edge of the corral were three more of the creatures, trotting in nervous circles on the stone floor, oblivious to the commotion at the iron gate. Beyond the coral, he saw several corpses in various states of mutilation, dangling from the metal rail on thick chains attached to their feet. The slaughter had ground to a halt when the men had fled to join the battle, and now it stood frozen, like some gruesome scene from the blackest nightmare.

Cade startled as a shadow suddenly cast over the corral, stepping forward from just beyond the hanging, butchered carcasses. The creatures squealed and snorted, digging their noses and sides into the iron gate, instinctively moving away from the approaching footsteps. From behind a half-carved corpse, Deacon stalked threateningly toward the corral. The sweat from his broad, bare chest gleamed in the flickering torchlight, and his face was grim and callous. His dead, black eyes pierced straight through the shadowy tunnel and fell squarely on Cade. As Deacon stepped to the edge of the corral, he reached down and unfastened the giant cleaver from his belt. The creatures were frenzied now, their legs kicking into the stone floor. Their snouts were gashed and bruised at their attempts to squeeze through the iron bars.

"You shouldn't have come here," said Deacon, his voice deep and malevolent. With his free hand, he opened the small gate at the other end of the corral and stepped in, closing it behind him. The boys quivered as they stood frozen behind the iron gate. As he approached, he swung the cleaver in menacing arcs, the blade whistling in the stale, putrid air of the stone chamber.

Cade searched desperately in the dark hallway for the lever to open the gate and free the creatures. His hands clawed frantically at the stones. Sebastian took a deep breath beside him as if to calm himself for what was to come. Then, he slid the jagged, wooden stick through the gate and jabbed it in the air to keep Deacon from the creatures.

"Hurry, Cade!" cried Sebastian, realizing the futility of his plan.

"I don't know where it is!" shouted Cade.

"Check back by the entrance!" bellowed Sebastian instinctively. "I'll try to keep him at bay...hurry!" he said, still poking his wooden stick vainly in the air.

Deacon was halfway across the corral now. The shrieks of the creatures pierced Sebastian's eardrums as they cried in terror at the approaching form. Cade sprinted down the hallway toward the entrance.

Suddenly, Robert turned and faced Deacon as the other creatures scratched and dug fruitlessly into the unforgiving stone. He would not lay down for the butcher without a fight.

Sebastian's eyes grew wide as Robert dug his hooves into the ground and charged. Deacon glanced down and saw Robert coming, raising his cleaver to strike at the charging creature, but Robert was upon him quickly, slamming headlong into his legs and sending him sprawling backward hard on the stone. Robert tumbled violently from the impact and slammed into the metal fence of the corral, falling to a heap. Deacon cursed and rolled to his feet, retrieving the cleaver that had clattered to the floor by his side. His face twisted into a foul sneer, and he walked slowly toward Robert's motionless form, lying by the far side of the corral.

Just then, the chains above the metal gate began to grind. The gate shuddered and started to rise slowly but then stopped, leaving only a small opening under which to pass.

"Higher!" shouted Sebastian frantically to Cade down the hall.

"It's stuck!" replied Cade, sounding distraught.

Wasting no more time, Sebastian dropped to the ground and rolled beneath the gate. The creatures on the other side pressed themselves against the stone floor and wriggled through the narrow opening, undaunted by the metal tips digging and cutting into their skin as they forced their way beneath. One by one, they disappeared down the black tunnel toward the meadow.

Robert trembled and then rolled upright; his eyes were glazed with fog. He shook his head and seemed to regain himself, setting eyes on Deacon once more, and then charged a second time. But Deacon was ready this time. At the last second, he stepped to his side, and Robert passed where he would have been. As he did, Deacon planted the heel of his boot in Robert's side and kicked him hard in the direction he was heading, sending him throttling along the stone and smashing headfirst into the metal corral. The wind expelled from him in a harsh groan as he crashed to the ground and went still.

Desperately, Sebastian wriggled his wiry frame under the gate and scrambled to his feet. He thrust the wooden stick before him bravely like a pike and charged at Deacon. From the corner of his eye, Deacon noticed the boy's charge and side-stepped the sharpened stick that went plunging just past his neck. As Sebastian passed, Deacon caught the end of the stick and yanked it from his hands, sending him tumbling awkwardly across the hard ground. His head slammed hard into the stone floor. Deacon scoffed in disgust at the splintered, wooden stick and tossed it across the corral as he stepped toward the fallen boy. The shadow of his hulking frame engulfed Sebastian's twisted body, lying crumpled on the cobbled floor. Fighting unconsciousness, Sebastian rolled on his back with a pained groan as his mind battled against the settling fog.

Deacon looked down at Sebastian and sneered, his lips curling downward in a sickening grimace. The stone building had grown cold and quiet now. On one end of the corral, Robert lay motionless against the iron fence. On the other, Sebastian barely raised himself off the ground, wobbling unsteadily on his elbows, as his mind roiled and spun, as if caught beneath the churning river rapids. Pacing toward Sebastian with slow, methodical strides, Deacon grasped the obsidian handle of his wicked cleaver and raised it high above the boy with both hands. His scowl twisted upward into a cruel smirk, his teeth the gray-brown hue of a sickly cadaver.

"Look at the trouble you've caused, boy," he hissed. The thick tendons on his muscled arms tensed as the cleaver rose toward the ceiling, arcing backward over his head for the final strike. "All over a bit of swine flesh…"

And then, the cold, dead silence of the slaughterhouse was splintered by the wet, sickly sound of punctured flesh. Deacon exhaled suddenly with a guttural grunt, and his eyes wrenched open wide, his jet black pupils flickering against the torchlight. His fingers slackened their vice-like grip on the massive cleaver, and it dropped to the stone floor, clattering loudly on its blade. Aghast, his eyes rolled downward and fixed on the end of the old, wooden stick rammed straight through his back and jutting from his thick, bare chest like the head of some bloody snake. He inhaled, his lungs wheezing a horrible croaking noise, then fell hard to his knees and smashed face-first into the unforgiving stone floor, the old, wooden stick still buried deep in his back.

Behind him, Cade stood trembling, his hands clenched as if still holding the stick. His heart pounded as he stood there frozen in a dreamlike state.

Sebastian tilted his head toward Cade and blinked deeply, his eyes still glassy. He braced his feet beneath him and tried to stand but tottered and wilted, falling roughly to the floor. His attempt pierced the veil of Cade's stupor, and he rushed toward Sebastian, dropping to his knees beside him. He lifted Sebastian's head from the hard ground and cradled it in his hands.

"You...you did it," Sebastian said, barely a whisper.

Cade shook his head gently as tears welled in his eyes. "No, Sebastian. We did it, friend."

Sebastian gathered himself once more and rose to his feet, leaning on Cade for support. He blinked and pressed his hands to his temple, pushing away the fog. "Robert," he said softly as he looked around the corral. In the distance, Robert lay where he fell, the faint rise and fall of his breath barely visible. Cade rushed across the corral to Robert's side with Sebastian ambling slowly behind him.

"He's alive," said Cade, resting his hand softly on Robert's side. A look of relief crossed Sebastian's face as he approached.

Then, Cade looked at Sebastian with a sudden realization. "Kirill," he said gravely. "Stay with Robert," he added and then jumped to his feet, rushing back toward the iron gate and pressing himself to the floor to slide through the narrow opening. Cade sprinted down the tunnel, barreling into the iron bars that sealed off the meadow. At his feet, the pink creatures stirred and scratched at the gate, anxious to escape the ominous stone building.

Cade pressed his face to the gate and looked into the meadow. In the far distance, he saw three wolves, their gray-brown coats smeared with blood. All around them, the corpses of villagers lay scattered like matchsticks, their satin shirts and woven pants torn wide over grisly wounds. The wolves circled a single man, the lone survivor of the villagers who had come to save the slaughterhouse. Across the meadow, Cade could see the villager's eyes glowing in terror like two moons set ablaze with the grim realization of his impending death.

Cade looked to his left, just beyond the gate. There on the ground lay Kirill's enormous body, his shaggy fur deeply matted and caked with dust and crusted patches of blood. From his side, a broken spear dangled hideously, its shaft quivering in a gentle wind that blew across the tall grass of the meadow. On his back, only the hilt of a sword was visible, the blade buried somewhere deep inside the great bear. Beside Kirill's body, two forms lay broken, barely recognizable as men. Their joints twisted grotesquely and ivory colored bones protruded from open wounds.

Cade fumbled feverishly against the stone wall for the lever and yanked it hard. The gate slowly started to rise, the metal chains winding torturously. Cade dropped to the ground and rolled beneath the rising gate, spinning to his feet and rushing to Kirill's side. As the heavy iron bars lifted, the pink creatures squirmed beneath and sprinted across the meadow, their thick legs carrying them into the woods until they vanished from sight.

Kirill was just barely alive. His eyes flickered beneath their eyelids, and his ragged breath blew warm across Cade's face. Cade pressed his face deeply into Kirill's side, his cheeks sinking deep into the matted fur. He could hear Kirill's lungs gurgling, like the wayward tendril of some forest stream, bubbling and dying among the dry rocks.

"Kirill," said Cade, desperately. "Kirill," he pleaded. The bear's eyelids quivered, and his eyes opened slightly. The glow in his amber eyes that had haunted the Elkin Forest for ages was now but a fading candle. Yet, even in the last vestiges of life, Cade could still sense the bear's magic — something otherworldly, something greater than the world of men. And now, Kirill was dying, and with him, the spirit of the forest was dying, too.

Cade buried his face in Kirill's fur. Beneath him, Kirill breathed deeply, in long, jagged breaths. His coarse fur bristled with the rising and falling of his lungs. And then, the great bear's eyes closed one final time, and his body fell still. In tears, Cade clung to Kirill's lifeless body like an orphan child to the corpse of his mother.

A small hand rested gently on Cade's shoulder.

"Kirill," said Sebastian softly in somber reverence. Cade raised his tear-stained face from Kirill's body and turned, looking at his friend. The pangs of guilt brewed and welled inside him as he lay there in the meadow.

Sebastian looked thoughtfully at Cade, absorbing the tragedy. Beside him, Robert stood in somber vigil. His deep, reflective eyes bore the unmistakable tenor of grief. His body bruised and bloodied from the slaughterhouse whips, Robert stood there unbroken, paying reverence to Kirill's sacrifice.

Several paces behind Sebastian and Robert, cloaked in the tall grass of the meadow, the big wolf and two others stood like phantoms. Though their fur was spattered with the blood of untold villagers, they looked tender and noble upon Kirill's body. The big wolf raised his head and looked at Cade, his eyes connecting inward with the boy. Wordlessly, the wolf paid his respects both to Kirill and to the battle of this day. Then slowly, he turned and trotted for the wood line, the other two wolves following his lead — and then they were gone into the forest.

As the breeze whistled across the meadow, rustling Kirill's fur, Robert stepped forward and gently nuzzled his snout against Cade's chest then leaned forward and sniffed at Kirill's body, inhaling deeply. Cade knew without question that Robert understood the magnitude of what had happened here.

After a moment, Cade stood and scanned the horizon. All around, the bloodied and broken bodies of men were strewn across the meadow. In the distance, soft wisps of gray smoke fluttered and mingled with the clouds as the dying embers of fallen torches burned small patches of tall grass. High overhead, a black fleck circled the battlefield, powerful, broad wings pulsing against the canopy of the deep blue sky. In the distance, the white birds stirred and squawked loudly in their cages, rattling desperately against the rusted metal.

"They should be free," said Sebastian softly, gazing toward the animals.

Cade stood for a moment in the quiet of the meadow. The crisp breeze swept across the battlefield, bending the tall grass in communion with the fallen bodies. Above, the faint hues of blue sky faded to velvety black, and the wispy clouds swallowed the final, drab plumes from the towering chimney over Marwol.

He looked down at Robert, standing quietly beside him. Beneath the blood and muck, Robert's eyes burned bright and alive. Reaching down, Cade hoisted Myrick's rusted sword from the grass and started across the meadow toward the cages.

THANK YOU

Thank you for taking the time to read this book. If you found this reading worthwhile, please consider leaving a review wherever you purchased the book. More reviews will help more readers find and appreciate this story.

If you would like to explore my other books and receive a free short story based on the events of "Chasing the Blue Sky," please visit:

www.lomackpublishing.com

Thank you again for giving up your valuable time to read this book. I hope you found the time well-spent.

~ WILL LOWREY

ABOUT THE AUTHOR

Will Lowrey is an attorney and animal rights advocate from Richmond, Virginia. He holds a Juris Doctor from Vermont Law School and a Bachelor of Science from Virginia Commonwealth University. For close to two decades, both before and after law school, Will has been actively involved in animal causes. His experiences include deployments to assist animals in disasters, the closure of roadside zoos, caring for animals from dog and cock fighting cases, community outreach for low income pet owners in areas ranging from urban neighborhoods to Native American reservations, animal rights protests, animal sheltering, public records campaigns against large institutions conducting animal research, and countless other adventures.

In 2018, Will founded Lomack Publishing to promote the rights, interests, and dignity of animals through self-published literature. Will is also the author of *"Chasing the Blue Sky"* and *"Words on a Killing"* through Lomack Publishing as well as *"We the Pit Bull: The Fate of Pit Bulls Under the United States Constitution"* published in the Lewis and Clark Animal Law Review Journal, Volume 24, Issue 2.

While most of Will's writing focuses on animal causes, he has dabbled in other areas, writing *"Simple Strategies for the Bar Exam,"* a guide for law students and attorneys taking the bar exam as well as *"The Tenebrous Mind,"* a collection of horror stories.

Will enjoys hearing from readers. If you'd like to contact him, please visit:

www.lomackpublishing.com